"I think you really liked the thought that I might be noticing you, finding you attractive,"

Brock said, then took Julia's chin in his thumb and index finger. "Otherwise your skin wouldn't be so pink or so warm."

"It's hot in here," she protested angrily, but to her credit, she didn't try to jerk away.

"You just told me you were cold. Your exact words were 'The dress makes me feel cold...and naked.' "

"Kind of have a one-track mind, don't you?"

He smiled, seeing the spark of attraction in her eyes, feeling it in the warmth of her skin. She couldn't hide it, no matter how hard she tried. In fact, the harder she tried, the more obvious it became.

Dear Reader,

What makes a man a Fabulous Father? For me, he's the man who married my single mother when she had three little kids (who all needed braces) and raised us as his own. And, to celebrate an upcoming anniversary of the Romance line's FABULOUS FATHERS series, I'd like to know *your* thoughts on what makes a man a Fabulous Father. Send me a brief (50 words) note with your name, city and state, giving me permission to publish all or portions of your note, and you just might see it printed on a special page.

Blessed with a baby—and a second chance at marriage—this month's FABULOUS FATHER also has to become a fabulous husband to his estranged wife in *Introducing Daddy* by Alaina Hawthorne.

"Will you marry me, in name only?" That's a woman's desperate question to the last of THE BEST MEN, Karen Rose Smith's miniseries, in *A Groom and a Promise*.

He drops her like a hot potato, then comes back with babies and wants her to be his nanny! Or so he says...in *Babies and a Blue-Eyed Man* by Myrna Mackenzie.

When a man has no memory and a woman needs an instant husband, she tells him a little white lie and presto! in *My Favorite Husband* by Sally Carleen.

She's a waitress who needs etiquette lessons in becoming a lady; he's a millionaire who likes her just the way she is in *Wife in Training* by Susan Meier.

Finally, Robin Wells is one of Silhouette's WOMEN TO WATCH—a new author debuting in the Romance line with *The Wedding Kiss*.

I hope you enjoy all our books this month—and every month!

Regards,

Melissa Senate,
Senior Editor

Please address questions and book requests to:
Silhouette Reader Service
U.S.: 3010 Walden Ave., P.O. Box 1325, Buffalo, NY 14269
Canadian: P.O. Box 609, Fort Erie, Ont. L2A 5X3

WIFE IN TRAINING

Susan Meier

Silhouette®

ROMANCE™

Published by Silhouette Books

America's Publisher of Contemporary Romance

For the inspiration for this book,
my nephew, the real Zachary

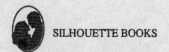

SILHOUETTE BOOKS

ISBN 0-373-19184-7

WIFE IN TRAINING

Copyright © 1996 by Linda Susan Meier

This edition published by arrangement with Harlequin Books S.A.

® and TM are trademarks of Harlequin Books S.A., used under license.
Trademarks indicated with ® are registered in the United States Patent
and Trademark Office, the Canadian Trade Marks Office and in other
countries.

Printed in U.S.A.

Books by Susan Meier

Silhouette Romance

Stand-in Mom #1022
Temporarily Hers #1109
Wife in Training #1184

Silhouette Desire

Take the Risk #567

SUSAN MEIER

has been an office manager, the division manager for a charitable organization and a columnist for a local newspaper. Presently, she holds a full-time job at a manufacturing company.

Even though her motto, "The harder you work, the luckier you get," is taped to the wall of her office, Susan firmly believes you have to balance work and play. An avid reader and lousy golfer, she has learned to juggle the demands of her job and family, while still pursuing a career in publishing and playing golf twice a week.

GOING FROM RAGS TO RICHES:

(or How To Marry Prince Charming)

1. Convince him that only *he* can give you a crash course on how to be proper—the proper wife, that is!

2. Come to your lessons with a sleepy, sexy look in your eyes. Because he'll be tempted to take you in his arms—and wonder about taking you to bed....

3. Let him think taking you and your son to the zoo is his idea—he'll be begging to be a part of the family in no time flat.

4. Love him—with all your heart!

Chapter One

The bedroom door slammed behind her. Julia MacKenzie gasped and spun away from the tall chest of drawers, but knew it was too late. "Zachary," she called, trying not to sound panic-stricken.

"Zachary, honey," she crooned, racing to the door and yanking it open. "Stay right where you are," she said, but even before the words tumbled from her lips she saw the hall was empty.

"Zack!" As she bounded into the corridor, she glimpsed a tiny pink foot disappearing behind the wall hiding the back steps. Like a heat-seeking missile, she zoomed after it. Having her three-year-old terror set free in this house full of treasures and antiques sent up all her nerves like a Fourth of July rocket.

By the time she reached the top of the steps, Zack was already at the bottom. "Wait for Mom," she called, but he only grinned up at her, his broad smile exposing his white teeth, his bright blue eyes sparkling with devilment, his chubby, newly bathed body as naked as the day he was born.

"If you don't wait for me, you're getting a time-out," she warned as she ran down the steps. But Zack only giggled and took off again.

In the first floor hall, Julia didn't even debate which way to turn. A normal kid would go straight to the family room, with the toys, the bar stocked with soda, the big-screen TV. But Zack wasn't really a normal kid. He was a clone of his father. Handsome as sin with his blue eyes and thick brown crew cut. An easygoing, yet hellishly devilish male, who loved teasing women—and, at three, that meant his mother.

Julia turned toward the white living room. The room with a white sofa, white rugs, antique tables and crystal lamps.

Two feet before she reached the living room door, Julia dropped to her knees. It was her only hope of getting to Zack before he spotted her and bolted again. Hidden by a chair's broad arm, she surveyed the room and saw Zachary patting the center cushion of the pristine white sofa. She breathed a sigh of relief, thanking God his hands were clean from the bath he'd had five minutes ago.

Julia silently crawled across the thick white carpeting to her son. She lunged and grabbed him around the belly, yelling, "Gotcha!"

But even before the "cha" was fully out, Julia saw a pair of incredibly shiny black loafers directly in front of Zachary. Those loafers were connected to argyle-covered ankles, which were connected to gray trousers, a charcoal-gray jacket, a white shirt, long neck, five-o'clock-shadowed chin. . . .

And the handsomest face on the planet.

Brock Roberts.

"Who the hell are you?"

Julia felt all the breath freeze in her lungs. Brock wasn't supposed to come home until his father's operation. Fear and apprehension turned her limbs to rubber. Zack took advantage of her momentary weakness and bounced out of her hold.

"Zack!" she yelped as he bounded away from her. Julia made one quick grab for him, but, being on her knees and slightly off balance, she missed, and Zack was gone again.

"What the..." Brock said, watching Zack as he scampered past his calves.

Julia scrambled to her feet. "Excuse me," she said, considering the preservation of the expensive furniture in the Roberts home much more important than protocol right now.

Apparently Brock agreed.

"I'll go this way," he said, pointing down the corridor that led to the study. "You go that way," he instructed, indicating the short hall that led to the kitchen or the family room, depending on whether you went straight or turned left, under the spiral staircase.

"Okay," she said, and dashed off on her appointed course. At the end of the hall, she peeked into the kitchen. Mrs. Thomas, a slight, thin woman with curly gray hair, stood by the butcher block, fussing over leftovers. "Have you seen Zack?" Julia asked breathlessly.

Mrs. Thomas grinned. "Got away from you again, did he?"

Julia nodded.

"Well, he's not in here."

"Thanks," Julia said, and pivoted toward the hall that led to the family room.

But he wasn't in the huge, quiet game room, either.

Panicking, she darted from the room. Zack was in the study. She knew it. He was in the room with the glass coffee tables and end tables. The leather sofa. The mahogany desk. The eight billion delicate knickknacks on bookshelves and assorted tables.

At the door of the study, she paused, took a deep breath for courage, then marched in. The scene that greeted her almost made her laugh. Standing in front of the grinning, naked three-year-old stood Brock Roberts. His arms were outstretched as if he were a guard blocking a basketball hoop, but because of Zack's size Brock's arms were too high, and Zack only laughed at the attempt to detain him.

"Zachary, come to Mommy," Julia said quietly, and, smiling, Zack scampered over to her. She dropped to one knee and would have scooped him off his feet, but he veered to the right, slipped past her and darted out the door.

"Damn," Julia muttered, and rushed after him.

"Damn," she heard Brock Roberts mutter as he followed her.

Zack eluded her in the two sitting rooms, but he set the lamps to rocking, knocked all the magazines off a table and left a handprint on the wall—how he'd gotten his hand dirty enough to make a handprint, Julia had no idea. At the moment she was only concerned with finding him.

Her fastest gait got her to within two feet of him, but he moved his shoulder at just the precise second as she reached for him, and she missed him again.

His little feet thumping on the tile of the hall, Zachary zipped away from them. Brock caught Julia's elbow in his strong hand and eased her out of his way. Then he began sprinting. He captured Zachary two seconds before Zack would have run straight into a curio cabinet filled with small glass ornaments.

Not even out of breath after their run through two halls and a huge, echoing foyer, Brock pivoted to face Julia. He used his right arm to support Zachary's chest, but Zack actually sat on Brock's left forearm. Her son's small lips had turned upward in a devilish grin; his blue eyes danced. But Brock Roberts didn't look nearly as happy as Zachary. In fact, the phrase "if looks could kill" immediately came to mind.

"Who are you?"

She swallowed. "I'm Julia MacKenzie. That's my son, Zack." At the mention of his name, Zack started to giggle. He twisted his neck until he could look up into Brock's face.

His expression clearly revealed his childlike respect for the man who could catch him with such ease. Brock Roberts neither noticed nor cared.

"What, exactly, are you doing in my house?"

"My house," Frank Roberts corrected him. Leaning heavily on his cane and dressed in navy-blue pajamas and a blue-and-gold paisley robe, he hobbled toward them. "And Julia's my nurse."

Slightly taken aback, Brock Roberts looked at her, then at Zack, then back at Julia again. He studied her wild red hair, her bright green eyes and her slender body. Before he returned his gaze to her face, Brock knew who she was.

"Very funny, Dad," he said quietly, handing squiggling, giggling Zachary to his mother. "But if I remember correctly this woman works for Moe...." He paused. "She's a waitress."

"Waitress. Practical nurse. There's really not a whole hell of a lot of difference," Frank said with a grunt as he made his way to the white sofa.

"Oh, really?" Brock said. "How about a couple years of schooling!"

"You told me to hire someone to keep me company, fluff my pillows, bring meals to my room," Frank said, patting the seat beside him. Without a word of instruction, Zack slid out of his mother's hold and hoisted himself up onto the cushion. Frank nestled the little boy against his side. "You don't need two years of school to do that. In fact, I actually think a waitress fits the bill a little better than a practical nurse does. And on top of all that, Julia plays a wicked game of pinochle." He smiled at her. "I already owe her fifty-two dollars and forty-three cents. We're playing for a penny a point."

Brock wasn't quite sure what was going on here, but the fact that this woman had his father playing cards for money sent all the wrong signals. Or maybe all the right signals. It was no wonder their business was going bankrupt. Everybody and his dog saw Frank Roberts as an easy mark.

Brock turned to Julia. "Ms. MacKenzie," he implored politely. "Would you give my father and me a few minutes alone?"

Looking almost grateful, Julia reached out for Zachary. "Sure."

Frank batted her hands away. "Let him stay here with me for a minute. I'll bring him up."

"You can't lift that little tub of lard!" Brock gasped.

"Now, wait a minute," Julia said. "Not only is my son a normal, healthy child, but you can't talk to your father that way."

"Calm down, Julia," Frank said, batting his hand again. "Brock's just a fussbudget, a worrywart. I don't lift him," Frank explained to his son. "I get Jeffrey to bring him up. So Zack's staying here. Julia deserves a few minutes of peace and quiet every day. I give her that when she takes her bath. Go ahead, Julia, I'll have Jeffrey bring Zack up in about a half hour."

Julia cleared her throat. "You're sure?"

"Of course I'm sure," Frank said kindly. "Just throw a pair of blanket sleepers and some training pants down the stairs and I'll dress him for bed."

"Okay. Good night, Frank," Julia said, and left the room.

"Frank?" Brock said, staring at his father. "You let her call you Frank?"

"I let Jeffrey call me Frank and I let Mrs. Thomas call me Frank. They only call me Mr. Roberts when you're here."

"You see what I mean, Dad," Brock said, raising his hands helplessly. He noted, oddly, that the chubby little boy beside his father not only watched every move he made, but seemed to be inordinately amused by him. Zack grinned up at Brock mercilessly. "This is exactly why I want you to start being more careful with how you run things when you get back to work," he added, ignoring the brown-haired bundle of joy who sat grinning at him as if he were a cartoon or a character from *Sesame Street*. "In the past few years you've gotten a little too generous."

"Why? Because I let two people who've worked for me for more than twenty years call me by my first name?"

"It's not just that," Brock began, but he reined back about ninety-eight percent of the things he wanted to say. Brock's brother, Ian, hadn't called on Frank when the creditors came knocking at the door, he'd called Brock. In Boston. At Compu-Soft. Right in the middle of a board meeting.

Frank didn't realize Roberts Industries was tumbling toward bankruptcy. Since Frank got ill, Brock and his brother decided to keep him in the dark about Roberts Industries' problems as much as possible.

Ian and Brock had agreed it was best for Frank to think Brock had returned home to be available during Frank's upcoming heart surgery. But to cover their bases, they told Frank Brock also wanted to "help out" at the company and might even come home a little early to do it.

If Brock succeeded in bringing the company under control again, Frank would never be the wiser. But that was going to be a little tricky. Especially with an over-protective waitress and her curious son living here. Not only did Brock have to dip into the family's personal assets to get the operating capital to set the company right, but once Roberts Industries was semistable he planned to take a loan against the business so he could make the necessary improvements to bring it into the twenty-first century.

He had no doubt that he could talk his father through most of his plans as long as he took it one step at a time. Brock simply didn't want the local waitress overhearing that his family was in dire straits and then reporting it to the community.

Which meant he had to get rid of her.

He took a seat on the sofa beside his father. Tilting his head, grinning like a fool, the little boy gazed up at him. Brock ignored him. "Dad," Brock said amicably, "I'm home early because *I* want to take care of you."

Frank grunted. "I thought you were coming home early to see if Ian needed any help at the factory."

"That, too," Brock agreed.

"So, while you're spending time at the plant, I still need Julia."

The little boy's grin widened as if he knew Frank Roberts had just won the first round.

Brock gave the child an arched look. The kid's grin grew even wider. Now his little white teeth were exposed.

"Actually, what I think you need is a practical nurse."

"And *I* think Julia does fine." Frank sighed heavily. "Besides, I made a bargain with her."

Brock exploded from the couch. "A bargain? What kind of bargain?"

"Good God, Brock," Frank said, exasperated. "It's a very good bargain. An even bargain. She's not ripping me off. Why are you making such a big deal out of this? The woman is competent. She's cheerful, pleasant to have around. If these are my last days, can't I at least have pleasant ones?"

"You're not going to *die*."

As Brock said those words, Zachary's eyes widened, and he twisted his head so that he could stare dumbstruck at Frank. Immediately Brock realized his comment had had exactly the opposite effect than he had intended—at least for Zachary. Instead of reassuring him, Brock had just scared the hell out of the poor kid.

"Let me go see if those training pants are at the bottom of the steps," Brock said as he rose from the couch. At the moment, dealing with the stricken look on the little boy's face was more important than getting to the bottom of his father's bargain with Julia MacKenzie. First, because Brock saw genuine fear in Zack's bright blue eyes. And second, because his father really was getting the better of him and Brock hoped this break in the action would clip Frank's momentum.

Brock grabbed Zack and hoisted him into his arms. "You certainly don't miss a meal."

"No, he's a healthy eater," Frank said, chuckling.

"We'll be back in two minutes."

As they walked down the hall, Brock could see the fuzzy blue sleepers lying at the foot of the steps. "I think I'm going to dress you right here so we can have a man-to-man talk," Brock said, and to his surprise Zack looked at him and said, "Okay."

"Oh, so you can talk," Brock said, astounded.

Zack gazed at him. "Uh-huh."

"Good." Brock directed Zack to step into a pair of plastic pants. "How old are you, kid?"

Zack grinned and held up three fingers. "Free."

"*Free.* Good. I didn't know kids could talk at *free,* but now that I think about it it makes perfect sense. And it also means that you probably see and understand a lot more than most adults think you do."

Zack only grinned.

Brock resisted the urge to ruffle his hair. The kid was so darned cute and so darned lovable it was hard to be angry with him—no matter how much furniture he'd almost destroyed. "Now, here's the deal. You see, my dad is a little sick, but he's going to be okay."

"Uh-huh."

"So I don't want you to worry."

Zack shook his head.

"And I don't want anything my dad says to scare you."

This time, Zack nodded his head. "Okay."

"When we go back into the living room you just hang in there with me as if nothing's wrong."

"Okay."

"Good."

They walked back down the hall together, hand in hand, but when they reached the white sofa Frank was sound asleep. Brock looked down at Zack, over at his father, and then back at Zack again. Unless Brock missed his guess, he'd just been handed the perfect opportunity to discuss this "bargain" with Ms. MacKenzie—without having to worry about his father's unstable condition or his interference.

Chapter Two

Hoisting Zachary into his arms again, Brock turned from the living room. He carried the child upstairs to the most frequently used guest room in the house and was gratified to see a light beneath the door. He knocked twice.

Without hesitation, Julia called, "Just bring him in, Jeffrey."

At the innocent and trusting tone of her voice, Brock felt a stab of guilt since he knew he wouldn't be as welcome as Jeffrey, the butler, would have been. He opened the door, anyway, then promptly stopped dead in his tracks.

This *definitely* was not a good idea.

Pulling back the brightly printed comforter on a child-size bed, Julia MacKenzie didn't look anything like the mother of a three-year-old. Her strawberry hair had been combed to the top of her head and fell in a ponytail of ringlets that reached her shoulders. Damp tendrils framed her face. Scrubbed of makeup, her skin looked as smooth and perfect as a new peach. Her gray T-shirt and hip-level sweatpants clung to her curves, but not intentionally. Brock knew that outfit would not have looked the same on any other woman on earth.

He cleared his throat. "I brought Zachary," he said, sounding sheepish and awkward, and inwardly cursing himself. *For heaven's sake,* he thought. *So she looks good in casual clothes. You're not interested, remember? You have other more important things on your mind.*

Yeah, right, his conscience argued, but Brock ignored it. After all, he had a mission, a purpose for coming up here. He didn't merely wish to deliver her child. He was getting to the bottom of her bargain with his father.

"Ms. MacKenzie," Brock said, and cleared his throat once. "I think you and I should have a talk."

"What about?" she asked, taking Zachary from his arms. "And it's Julia," she added as she sat on the rocker by the bay window of the huge room. The floral comforter of the four-poster bed had also been turned down. A book lay open on the cherry-wood bedside table. Obviously, she'd been reading. For some reason or another that thought struck him as oddly as the fact that she had a nearly perfect figure beneath all that gray fleece.

"I was wondering about this bargain you've made with my father."

She glanced at him, her green eyes innocent. "He didn't explain it to you?"

Brock shook his head. "He fell asleep."

Taking a long, deep breath, Julia nestled Zachary against her bosom.

Brock realized he was staring at her breasts and quickly looked away. *This* was getting ridiculous.

"Actually, Mr. Roberts, it's quite simple. Just like he told you, he needs someone to keep him company while he recovers from his pneumonia, and then for a few weeks after his surgery."

She paused. Brock waited. When she didn't offer any further explanation, Brock asked, "And you get what in return?"

"Well, he's paying me," Julia admitted, and from her reluctance Brock knew there was more.

"And?"

"And he's sort of helping me with Zachary."

"How?" Brock asked, growing more comfortable because he was in familiar territory. Holding a three-year-old, watching a mother, those weren't his forte. Pulling information about a bargain was. Negotiating was. Arbitrating companies out of bad decisions was.

"Look," she said, her breath coming out in a slow stream. "This is a long story."

"I have time," Brock said, leaning against the cherry-wood armoire.

"I don't," she countered. Glancing down at her squirming child, she added, "If I don't start reading to him within the next five minutes, I won't have him asleep until midnight."

"Then make your explanation short."

She sighed. "All right. Zack's a little rambunctious."

"No kidding."

"He also hasn't ever been around nice things."

"And you want to live here for a few weeks so he can see how the other half lives?" Brock asked, confused.

Julia started to laugh. The music of her voice filled the room. "I hadn't quite thought of it that way, but yes. That's exactly it."

Brock pulled away from the tall chest. "I'm sorry, Ms. MacKenzie, but given my father's condition and given that your end of the bargain borders on the ridiculous, I'm afraid I'm going to have to ask you to dissolve this agreement."

"What?"

"At best, you have a fanciful arrangement, something created to make my father feel generous and to give you a chance to live in a nice house. At worst, I have a very sick father, who really is going to need a nurse when he gets out of the hospital after his surgery, and you're not a nurse. I understand both your intentions and my father's intentions were good, but neither was practical. So I'm asking you to leave."

"I can't leave!" she said, and virtually sprang from the chair. Clutching Zachary, she bounded toward him. "Your father made a deal with me."

"And I intend to keep it."

Hearing his father's voice, Brock turned. From the redness of Frank's face and his labored breathing, Brock could tell the climb up the stairs had been difficult for him. And being angry wasn't helping him.

"Dad," Brock said, almost leaping to his aid, but his father batted him away.

"Zachary needs training for a few weeks to learn how to behave when he visits his paternal grandparents. I said we'd train him."

"But you're in no condition..."

"I'm about to have bypass surgery, Brock. Millions of people have this operation every year."

"And when you come out you'll need a practical nurse."

"No, I won't," Frank insisted. "Would you please think for a minute? Do you believe everybody who has this operation can afford to hire a practical nurse? Of course not. Yet they still survive."

When Brock didn't respond, Frank continued, "Don't you think it will be better to have someone to keep my spirits up than to have someone who knows how to give me shots I don't need?"

As Frank said the last, he glanced at Julia and she smiled at him. Brock's eyes narrowed. There was more to this, much more to this, than met the eye. But this was not the time to pursue it.

"All right, Dad," Brock said, taking his father's upper arms in his hand and turning him toward the door again. "Whatever you say."

After guiding his father through the doorway, Brock shifted slightly so that he could glance at Julia MacKenzie. She stood by the rocker, holding her bouncing bruiser, looking perfectly pleased with herself.

Well, he wasn't through with her yet.

"He wants my what?" Julia asked, confused.

"He requires your presence at breakfast, ma'am," Jeffrey said, the soft, cultured tones of his voice drifting to Julia over the phone.

"But it's six o'clock!"

"Mr. Roberts leaves for the office before seven. Breakfast is in five minutes."

Combing her hair out of her eyes, Julia listened to the sound of Jeffrey replacing his phone receiver. She followed suit, then rolled out of bed, dragging herself to the shower. She stood under the spray for two minutes before she realized that the perfect form of rebellion would have been to come as she was to this mandatory breakfast. Which was exactly what she intended to do.

She pulled off her shower cap, fluffed her hair by shaking it and then toweled herself dry. Only because she'd showered, she put on a clean sweater and jeans. And only because it would be barbaric to do otherwise, she brushed her teeth.

When she arrived downstairs, she was barefoot, her hair was as wild as a lion cub, her face as fresh and natural as the first rays of sunrise.

Jeffrey greeted her at the bottom of the back steps. "I'm afraid you're in the formal dining room this morning, Ms. Julia."

"I am?" she asked, glancing down past her thick mint-green sweater and loose-fitting jeans to her pink toes. She wiggled them, and considered returning upstairs for shoes, then decided that a rebellion was a rebellion, and followed Jeffrey to the dining room.

They reached the double-door entrance of the huge room, and Jeffrey pulled open both doors simultaneously. "Ms. Julia MacKenzie," he announced as the doors swung open.

Awestruck, Julia only stared at the short, balding butler. She'd been living in this house for two full weeks and not once... never... had he announced her. Suddenly, unexplainably, she felt like Elly May from *The Beverly Hillbillies.*

At the head of the table, Brock Roberts rose. He wore a charcoal gray suit similar to the one he'd worn the day before, but today his tie was red, the hankie in his breast pocket was red, and his shirt was pristine white. With his dark eyes, dark hair and brooding good looks, he looked like a member of a royal family—at the very least he looked like the prince from books she'd read to Zachary.

"Well, good morning, Ms. MacKenzie. How nice of you to dress for breakfast."

"How nice of you to give me five minutes' notice that I was dining with you," Julia countered as he pulled out a chair for her and she sat.

"Ah, yes, I know how time-consuming it is to slide your feet into a pair of slippers. Juice?"

She gritted her teeth to calm herself before she answered, "Yes, please." ·

Brock himself poured her juice from an odd-looking vessel, which sat on a serving cart beside him. The same cart held a silver coffee service. Gold-trimmed dishes with a raised floral border provided a utilitarian decoration. The flatware beside her dish looked to be more expensive than Julia's rent payment.

Julia's heart began to pound. When they didn't eat with Frank, she and Zachary ate in the small breakfast nook, a sunny area surrounded by windows. They'd used dishes that were pretty, but normal. In fact, they reminded her of her own dishes. The glasses they'd used were simple, not crystal like these. Their flatware had been limited, not lined up in a merciless row.

Brock handed her the glass, and she stared at it. Seeing him reach for a second glass, which she assumed he'd pour for himself, Julia took a cautious sip to stall for time. When he set his glass beside his plate, Julia mimicked the movement, then sighed with relief because he didn't seem to notice that she'd just copied him.

"Now, about this agreement you have with my father," he said, handing her a basket filled with muffins. Pursing her lips, she shook her head. He pulled the basket back, extracted a muffin for himself and set it on the small dish angled away from his plate. "I know that I came on a little strong last night. I apologize."

In spite of the fact that Julia knew Brock was about to kick her out again, she had to admit he did it with style. His smooth voice drifted over her. His nice words and perfect phraseology soothed her. Of course, that was exactly why he'd made the word choices he had. To lull her into the kind of state where she wouldn't fight him tooth and nail for what was rightfully hers.

She straightened her spine, determined not to let him get the best of her, though she didn't have much of a leg to stand on. The deal she'd made with Frank was verbal... and silly.

"After our discussion I realized that you probably had very little to do with this arrangement." He smiled. Mesmerized by his gorgeous coffee-colored eyes, his straight nose, high cheek-bones and his beautiful smile, Julia only stared at him.

"Since Moe—your employer," he explained unnecessarily, "and my father have been best friends since grade school, I'd bet this is a little scheme they cooked up themselves."

She nodded. "Moe mentioned to me that your dad needed someone to care for him."

"And I'll bet Moe mentioned to my dad that you needed someone to help you with Zachary."

As Brock said the last, Jeffrey entered carrying two plates. Each contained two eggs, a few strips of bacon and two pancakes.

"Thank you, Jeffrey," Brock said.

Julia quickly looked up at him. "Yes, thank you, Jeffrey," she added, ashamed that she'd made such a foolish mistake. She was a waitress, for Pete's sake. She knew to thank the person who served the food. Brock Roberts was starting to unnerve her.

She waited until he reached for a fork, saw he didn't do anything special or unusual, and realized she could eat without watching every move he made.

"Coffee?" Brock asked.

She glanced up. "Yes . . . please."

He looked at Jeffrey. "Jeffrey?"

"Very good, sir."

This time Julia immediately thanked Jeffrey. He offered an encouraging smile, and she sensed he knew how nervous and out of place she felt, even if Brock didn't.

"I'll have coffee, also, Jeffrey, then Ms. MacKenzie and I will take it from here."

Jeffrey poured Brock's coffee and left.

"I think I might have improperly given you the impression last night that I somehow thought you were to blame, that you'd coerced my father into making a deal that was unsuitable for his needs."

Brock set his fork on the edge of his plate and reached for his muffin. He split it and buttered only a small piece, which he put into his mouth.

Julia stared at him. With his dark skin and dark eyes, his looks were picture perfect. But his manners and charm actually took him beyond perfect. He really was like a prince out of Zachary's storybooks.

Shaking her head to break the spell, Julia came out of her daze. She needed to put things back into perspective. So what if Brock was incredibly polished and undeniably handsome? Big deal. No matter how nice he looked when he said it or how perfectly he phrased the request, Brock Roberts was still firing her.

"I don't think this deal is unsuitable for your father's needs."

"Surely, Ms. MacKenzie..."

It hit her, with the use of the word *surely*—that refined, yet condescending word that skittered up her spine the same way the winter wind did after it crawled beneath the hem of her old winter coat—that *this,* this type of person, this kind of dining, this environment, was exactly what she was about to encounter when she took Zack to Connecticut.

And she wasn't ready.

Not only was Zack a far cry from being prepared to spend two weeks in the mansion of a family so wealthy their estate had a guard, but *she* wasn't ready. If anything, Brock Roberts had just defeated his own purpose. He'd just pointed out how desperately *she* needed to be in this house. *She* needed training every bit as much as Zachary did.

"Excuse me, Mr. Roberts," she said calmly, though inside she felt a strange quaking, as the full import of her problems began to hit her. She would be on trial every bit as much as Zack would be, yet she'd never realized how short of the mark she fell, how totally unprepared she was until this very minute. There was no way she could leave this house, this opportunity to learn, and no way she was letting Brock Roberts get the best of her. "But your father and I have a deal. I intend to see to it that I uphold my end. Your father has every intention of keeping up his end."

She drew a breath and pushed herself away from the table. "So why don't you stay out of it?"

Chapter Three

Furious, Brock slammed his car into the Roberts Industries parking lot. He stormed into the front entryway, ran up the steps and barged into his father's office. No one questioned his presence. He was the golden boy. He'd not only gone to an Ivy League college, he'd also taken a dying computer company in Boston and turned it around in only five years. Now that he had decided to show an interest in his family's company, everyone knew it would only be to take complete control. Which was exactly what he was doing.

"Brock!" Ian greeted his brother as Brock threw his briefcase onto their father's desk.

"We have a problem," Brock said without preamble. "Close the door."

Ian, a shorter, rounder version of Brock, did as he was told, then sat on one of the two leather chairs in front of Frank's desk. "So what's up?"

"Dad has a roommate."

Ian's brow puckered. "A roommate?"

"He's got a woman living with him, acting as a practical nurse."

"So?"

"So, she's not a practical nurse, she's a waitress. She's one of *Moe's* waitresses."

"Which one?"

"Julia MacKenzie."

"Julia MacKenzie is Dad's practical nurse?"

"Got it in one," Brock said.

"I don't understand," Ian mumbled, shaking his head as if totally confused, and Brock certainly didn't blame him. The situation confused him, too.

"I don't understand, either, Ian," Brock said. "And I couldn't really get a straight answer out of Dad or Ms. MacKenzie last night or this morning. All I know is that she and Dad made some kind of bargain. Julia's not foolish enough to throw it away without a fight, and Dad's hell-bent on keeping his end." He paused, sighing. "And I do mean hell-bent. It's almost as if we owe her something."

"Oh, boy."

Brock glared at his younger brother. "Oh, boy, what?" he asked angrily.

Ian swallowed. "Well, Brock, we do sort of owe her."

"How?" Brock demanded.

"Well," Ian said, obviously stalling for time. "You see, Julia and I were neck and neck the whole way through high school for the Gertrude Penmore Scholarship."

"And?"

"And I cheated in my senior year to ensure that I'd get it."

"What!" Brock yelped. "Of all the stupid—"

"Oh, come on, Brock," Ian said. "Put yourself in my place. Not only was I young and impulsive, but I had an older brother making the dean's list at Princeton. You're sort of a tough act to follow. It was the only way I thought I could impress Dad."

"That's no excuse," Brock said, his eyes flashing fire. "Look how it's come back to haunt us!"

"Brock, you don't know anything about how this has haunted us. It's haunted us in a million ways for the past seven years. Though I never realized it at the time, I cheated Julia out of her only chance for a decent life. Not only did Julia's mother die right after we graduated, but now she's supporting a child—on a waitress's salary. Her luck's been nothing but bad, but she absolutely wouldn't hear of taking anything from us to make up for my mistake—not even money for her brother's education. If Dad believes he's finally found a way to pay her back, it's actually good news for us."

"So you agree with Dad, that she should stay?"

Ian thought a minute, then said, "Yeah, I agree with him."

"But you don't even know for sure that she's there because Dad's somehow paying her back."

"You can bet Dad's finding or has found a way to pay her back," Ian said confidently. "And I for one don't think we should stop him."

Brock only stared at Ian, then he bounced from his seat and began to pace. "Damn it, Ian, I can't go in and ask Dad to sign a power of attorney as long as that woman's snooping around. And we can't get a loan for improvements to the company without a power of attorney." He picked up a pencil and absently tapped the smooth shaft against his palm as he walked around the room. "Worse, I'm certainly not going to try to talk Dad into selling off assets until she's gone. Not only do I not want to have to explain to him publicly that we're selling property to pay past-due debts, but the very last thing we need is for her to get wind of the fact that we're liquidating some of the family's personal wealth. If she takes that news back into town with her it'll be twenty-four hours before the entire population of Roberts Run knows the company's in financial trouble."

"Then, ask Dad what his deal with her is, and meet our end of it the quickest way possible so that you can get her out of the house in the shortest amount of time."

"Our end of it seems to be house-training her overactive three-year-old."

"Zachary?"

"Yes," Brock said, plopping into his father's huge leather chair again. "The kid's cute, but he's bad, and I'm telling you, Ian, it's going to take more than six weeks of living in our house to tame him."

"Then, don't tame him. Tame her."

Brock only stared at Ian.

"I mean it. Maybe it's not Zachary who needs to get comfortable in a house like ours, maybe it's Julia."

This time, Brock gave his brother a thoughtful look. "Go on."

"Well, rumor has it that Zachary's father was really wealthy...like megawealthy."

"Then how'd he meet Julia?" Brock asked.

"He was a geologist, working for that strip mine company just across the county line, and he used to come into the diner for lunch. Anyway, I don't think anybody really understood how much money his family had until his parents tracked Julia down a few weeks ago. They sent half a law firm to the diner and served her with all kinds of papers. Moe had a lawyer friend who managed to barter Julia's way into a private meeting between her and Zachary's grandparents before any suits are actually filed. I think," Ian added uncertainly, "that the bottom line to this deal is that if the grandparents don't think Zack's being properly cared for, they're going to start custody proceedings."

Brock's face crumpled. "That stinks."

"That's probably why Dad thinks taming Zachary is the perfect payback."

* * *

Julia refused Brock's offer of dinner that night but couldn't escape another confrontation in the family room. Gathering Zack's toys, Julia again saw his feet first—brown loafers and argyle socks—and quickly stood.

"I'm sorry, Mr. Roberts," she said, apologetic but not soft or fearful. She had as much right in this house as he did—odd though that seemed—and he wasn't intimidating her out of it. Nonetheless, she did feel obliged to offer an explanation. "But Frank...your father...typically lets Zack do whatever he wants in this room. I straighten up once Zack's asleep."

To her surprise, Brock smiled at her. "That's actually an excellent idea."

Her eyes narrowed.

"Well, it seems to me that if we let him do whatever he wants in at least one room, he'll pretty much leave the other rooms alone."

"Not always," Julia said cautiously, "but most of the time." She had no idea what Brock was up to, but she no longer heard that disapproving tone in his voice. And she didn't think he was about to toss her out on her ear. Awkwardly, she toyed with her ponytail. Even though she had on the same jeans and sweater she'd worn to breakfast, she didn't feel completely unkempt as she had that morning— her hair was neatly tied away from her face and she was wearing clean white sneakers. But there was a part of her that always wished to look a little better when he was around. If only because he looked so damned good.

All things considered, Brock Roberts had to be the most attractive man on the face of the earth. His rust red cable knit sweater complemented his eyes so well that they nei- ther looked amber nor coffee; they were black, almost as black as his naturally wavy hair. His hands were strong, full and powerful, unlike the thin and wiry ones she would have expected from a chief executive officer from Boston.

Pushed-up sweater sleeves revealed a peppering of black hairs on muscular forearms that gave him the look of a longshoreman. Yet, he was sophisticated. Sharp and smart. You could see that in his eyes. The rumor mill had his big-city salary pegged at six figures. Judging from the Porsche sitting in front of the Roberts house right now, Julia assumed that theory had to be darned close to the truth.

"Look, Julia, I'm going to apologize one more time for my behavior."

"And then you're going to explain to me why I should go, right?"

"No," he said simply. "Actually, what I was going to suggest was that if you feel uncomfortable about dining with me it might be because I usually dress for meals."

Even though she'd only known him two days, she had grown accustomed to his look, his style. Dressed as he was in crisply pleated brown slacks and his thick, homey sweater, he managed to combine sophistication with pure sex appeal, and Julia rather enjoyed having him dress the way he did. Actually, she liked looking at him. She never would have believed that to be true, particularly since Zack's father had been a woodsy outdoorsman who wore jeans, plaid shirts and hiking boots. In fact, she hadn't even realized David was rich until it was too late. But the truth of the matter was, Brock Roberts appealed to her, exactly as he was, if only as an object for her optical appreciation.

It almost seemed sacrilegious to even consider that he'd dress down to her level.

"So now you're going to start wearing jeans?" she asked, managing only barely to keep the disappointment out of her voice.

"No," Brock said, "I was thinking more along the lines of your borrowing a few of my sister Angel's things for dining while you're here."

"I couldn't do that," Julia immediately refused, pride taking over before she even had a chance to think the situation through.

"Now, don't say that before you hear me out," Brock said, comfortably sitting on the arm of the floral sofa. "My father retires to his room early every night. Zack eats on his own schedule. There's no reason under the sun to make Jeffrey and Mrs. Thomas serve individual dinners for us, too."

What he said made a great deal of sense to Julia, but despite her initial protest Julia also knew his suggestion had even more merit than saving the staff extra work. She *needed* to spend time in that huge dining room, getting comfortable, adjusting to the table layout, learning how to eat food that required a little more sophistication than Moe's hamburgers. Sharing meals with Brock could be her perfect opportunity.

"I don't mind eating in the dining room with you," she said slowly. "I just don't see why you need for me to be wearing your sister's clothes."

"I think *you'd* be more comfortable," he stated emphatically as he rose from his seat, but Julia sensed her wearing those clothes was somehow more for his benefit than hers.

Still, appeasing him by wearing his sister's clothes almost seemed a small price to pay for the chance to sharpen her etiquette skills in the Roberts dining room. In fact, she even started to see some merit in the clothes idea, too. After all, she knew she'd be buying a new wardrobe with part of the money Frank was paying her. She had to look smart and capable. Right now, she only had clothes that said poor and struggling. Maybe wearing his sister's clothes would give her a better idea of what to buy for herself. Or, at least, an idea of what was comfortable and what wasn't.

"All right," Julia decided. "I'll borrow some of your sister's clothes."

"Great!" Brock said, leading her to the open doorway of the family room. "Let's go take a look.

"The one thing about Angel," Brock said as he pushed open the door to his older sister's former room, "is that she's a classic."

The huge, quiet bedroom was exactly what Julia had expected. The furniture was thick, heavy wood, much like the furniture in the rest of the house. A navy blue rug lay in the center of the hardwood floor. But the comforter on the double bed was light purple, almost lilac, the curtains eyelet lace and the throw pillows lilac and cream-colored satin.

The room was exactly what she'd expected. What she hadn't expected was Brock Roberts's sudden change of heart. If he'd suggested she try on his sister's clothes to intimidate her, he'd made a big mistake. Not only was she starting to really like the idea of using Angel's clothes to plan her own new wardrobe, but getting comfortable in the dining room was an added bonus. So, if he was trying to trick her, he was in for a shock. Because not only was she ready, willing and able to dip into his sister's wardrobe, but she wasn't leaving. He could embarrass her all he wanted. She'd simply take it as practice for meeting David's parents.

From the picture on the vanity, Julia could see what Brock meant about Angel being a classic with her blond hair styled in a modest page boy, and her trim body dressed in an oxford-cloth shirt, tweed jacket and jeans. Though slightly above average as far as attractiveness was concerned, Angel was slightly below average weight for her height—much like Julia—and for a woman who could afford almost anything, her taste in clothes appeared to be proper, unassuming.

Julia followed Brock to the closet. As she expected, all the clothing was unpretentious yet elegant. Even the evening dresses were classically cut, simple clothes, in spite of a few bangles and sequins. There were several different colors of pumps, a pair of loafers and an old pair of tennis shoes in the shoe rack.

"Here," Brock said, pulling out a black velvet dress. "Why don't we start by having you try this on?"

Julia's mouth dropped open and she looked at him. "What?" she said, but it came out more as a gasp.

"Try this on."

Though the dress was nothing but a straight black sheath, it was the most beautiful thing Julia had ever seen. The velvet looked as soft as baby's hair, and it had enough of a shine to it that it could have been lightly coated with glitter. She wasn't even sure she should risk touching it, let alone trying it on.

"I can't."

Brock looked at her as if she were crazy, then comprehension dawned. "Oh, I get it," he said, and pointed to a door at the right. "That's a bathroom. You can go in there for privacy."

She shook her head furiously. "No, you don't understand. I can't come in here and try on your sister's *best* clothes."

"She won't care."

"But I do."

"Oh, come on," Brock cajoled. "It's not that big a deal. I'll tell you what, if it will make you feel any better, we'll call Angel tomorrow, and not only will you see that she won't care if you try these things on, but I'll bet she tells you you can keep anything you want."

"*Keep* anything I want?" Julia asked, her eyes huge with disbelief.

"Sure, she doesn't need most of them in California, anyway," Brock said. He turned away and grabbed another dress. "How about this spangled thing?"

"This spangled thing" was a multi-colored sequined dress. The cap sleeves and turtleneck were the perfect foil for the long skirt which was slit from floor to the knee.

"But—" Julia protested.

Brock cut her off. "Julia, Angel left these things here when she went to California. She's probably forgotten she even owns them."

Awestruck, Julia stared at the closet full of clothes, knowing that someone had simply discarded them like yesterday's newspaper. As Brock watched her, he began to feel incredibly guilty. He'd never seen anyone so dumbfounded by things he'd always taken for granted. From the events of the past three minutes, Brock was beginning to understand why his father and Ian were so set on helping her.

Unconsciously, Brock took a step back, out of the way, as Julia took her first cautious step toward the closet. Sitting on the bed, he watched her as she poked through the racks, gasping with appreciation and awe every couple of seconds.

Suddenly, unexpectedly, she turned to him. "I know you probably think I'm a fool for being so impressed about something as stupid as dresses...."

"No," Brock assured her quietly, compassionately, but she went on as if she hadn't even heard him.

"It's just that my dad ran away right after my brother was born, and he more or less left us to fend for ourselves." Breaking eye contact, she turned and began to poke in the closet again. Pulling a dress from the rack and examining it as she held the soft garment against herself, she said, "We were doing okay until our mother died. Then the real trouble started."

She paused to draw another dress from the closet and turned away from him, toward a mirror. Though she could see him in the glass if she wanted, and he could definitely see her in the glass, she never looked at him. Brock began to realize she was almost hiding behind the clothes as she told her story.

"Having to support Tim made me realize that maybe my little family hadn't being doing so well, after all, all those years. I realized that my mother kept the bad things from me and Tim, and shouldered the burden alone.''

The sad but honest tone of her voice had the effect of a knife in Brock's chest, but as quickly as she'd turned introspective, she brightened. ''I like this one,'' she said happily. ''I've never worn much black, but I think this one might really look good on me.''

''So do I,'' Brock agreed. ''Why don't you go try it on?''

She walked into the bathroom and Brock noticed that she'd left the black velvet dress, the dress she really liked. It lay on the back of a chair. He reached for it, squeezed the soft velvet between his fingers, and an odd, tingling feeling engulfed him. Brock was torn between the guilt for wanting to be rid of her and double the guilt for not seeing sooner how hard her life had been. In these next couple of weeks, he, Brock Roberts, had a chance to change her destiny, and all he could think about was making sure his own needs were met.

Julia came out of the bathroom looking like a vision in the strapless black crepe dress she had chosen, but Brock knew she was meant for the velvet.

''You're beautiful. Perfect,'' he whispered, his voice coming out as soft as a cloud. After breakfast with the wild woman this morning, he'd almost forgotten she could be this beautiful—this breathtaking. Seeing her dressed like this was an easy reminder that there was much more to this woman than she let people see.

''Yeah, well, I don't like it,'' she said, eyeing herself critically in the full-length mirror. ''I feel cold. And naked. How do you keep one of these things up, anyway?'' As if to emphasize her point, she gave the top of the dress a mighty tug.

Brock smiled. Her rough-around-the-edges personality was starting to grow on him. He'd always hated pretentious people and admired honesty. Lately, he found too much of one and not enough of the other in his business dealings. It was only natural that once he got past the conflict of needing to be rid of her, Brock would find Julia as refreshing as a swim in Johnson's Creek. "I haven't the vaguest idea," he said, then reached out and casually took the black velvet dress from the chair. "Here, this one's got all its pieces. Why not try it?"

"That one?" she said suspiciously. "Why would I want to wear that thing?"

"Well, for one, it's got sleeves and a whole top," he said, again casually, not letting on that he knew this was the one she really wanted. "If nothing else, I'm absolutely positive you can even wear a bra with this one."

"You can tell I'm not wearing a bra?" she gasped, and covered herself with her forearms.

"Oh, for Pete's sake," Brock said, not quite sure if she was serious or teasing. Not about to take any chances, he took a quick look into her eyes and realized she wasn't only serious, she was mad. He almost couldn't believe it. "What difference does it make?"

"It makes a hell of a difference to me, knowing that you're standing there gawking at me!"

Her quaintness quickly began to lose appeal, but Brock refused to lose his composure. "I am not gawking at you," he patiently explained. "It's just that that dress doesn't have shoulders and I don't see any straps, so I'm *assuming* you're not wearing a bra."

"You're looking."

She said it with such absolute and condemning authority that Brock felt a nerve jump in his neck. His composure packed its bags and left him. "A little vain, aren't we?"

"No. If any one of us is anything, I'd say that one of us is a little perverted."

"Perverted? You think that noticing that a woman isn't wearing a bra is perverted?" He couldn't help it, he started to laugh. He took the four or five steps across the room and stood in front of her. "I know men who make a pastime out of noticing, and women who'd be sorely disappointed if men didn't notice. Don't you think perverted's a little strong?''

"Okay, you're right. *Juvenile's* a better word."

Incredulous that she would be so insulting over something so silly, he stared at her. "Juvenile?"

"Juvenile, immature, childish. Take your pick, I think they all apply."

With her last insult, the light dawned for Brock, and he realized that maybe she wasn't so honest, after all. "You want to know what I think?" he asked, stepping in front of her when she moved toward the bathroom door again. "I think you liked it."

"Liked it?"

"Really liked the thought that I might be noticing you. Finding you attractive," he said, then took her chin in his thumb and index finger. Her skin was smooth like the velvet of the dress she'd refused, warm as a summer night, and bright as a midday sun. "Otherwise, your skin wouldn't be so pink or so warm."

"It's hot in here," she protested angrily, but to her credit, she didn't try to jerk away.

"You just told me you were cold. Your exact words were that the dress made you feel cold...and naked."

"Kind of have a one-track mind, don't you?"

He smiled, filled with delight at the thought that she found him as attractive as he found her, but that he at least had the courage to admit it. He saw the spark of attraction in her eyes, felt it in the warmth of her skin. She couldn't hide it, no matter how hard she tried. In fact, the harder she tried, the more obvious it became.

"I think it's you who has the one-track mind," he disagreed, then bent his head and kissed her.

He put his hands on her shoulders to ensure that she stayed right where she was, but Julia felt the warmth of his fingers more as rippling waves. The smooth softness of his mouth on hers was nothing compared to the tingles of anticipation that were part fear that he was touching her so intimately, and part joyous reward that he found her attractive enough to kiss her. She knew it didn't mean anything, couldn't mean anything, not merely because their worlds were so different but more because their personalities just plain didn't mix. But, Lord above, kissing him was pure heaven.

She supposed it was the risk involved—the sure knowledge that they shouldn't be doing this—that made kissing him as wonderfully decadent as eating an ice cream sundae in bed after midnight.

She felt a yearning so deep inside of her that she would have sworn it was a stirring of her soul. An awakening that was part reminder of things from her past and new awareness of rare delights very few people experienced. But, just as quickly, the beauty of discovery turned into the stark reality of pure wanting. Desire so intense it was startling. The warmth and intimacy of his mouth on hers, the odd sensation of being pressed against him, and the contact of his body as it molded to hers, almost clung to hers, overwhelmed her, enveloped her, covered her with tingles from the top of her head to the tips of her feet.

She felt scared and happy both at the same time. She felt buoyant and light, yet weighted down by heavy limbs she knew she couldn't move if she wanted to.

She felt too much, too soon. Particularly for a man she not only couldn't have, but a man she actually didn't want. Though David and Brock were nothing alike, they shared one obvious common denominator. They were both too wealthy for their own good. In spite of the fact that David had shunned his wealth, he was part of a life-style that reached much further than Julia had ever suspected. Any doubts about that had been swept away when David's parents began to pursue Zachary. It would be foolish, downright absurd, to put herself in the same kind of situation twice. Which was exactly what she'd be doing if she decided to get involved with Brock Roberts.

"That's enough," she said, breaking the kiss and stepping away from him, effectively declining the relationship. Difficult though it was, she also had to decline the etiquette lessons and hope to pick up enough of everything she needed to know on her own, or from Frank. Because she wasn't even going to risk being in the same room with another man who could break her heart. "Thank you very much for the offer of the clothes," she said, then scooped her blue jeans and sweater from the floor of the bathroom. "But I don't think I'll be needing them."

Chapter Four

"**Y**ou did what?"

"I kissed her," Brock mumbled, and threw his pencil to his desk. "Then she told me she wasn't going to be needing Angel's clothes, which I took to mean I could pretty much forget my suggestion about us eating dinner together."

Ian shook his head. "You know, Brock, for someone who's won as many academic awards as you have, you sure can be stupid sometimes."

"It's a little late to cry over spilled milk," Brock said. "What we have to do is come up with another angle for me to use to try to get her involved in some kind of lessons."

"You're on your own," Ian said, rising from his seat. "We thought of the perfect plan yesterday and you blew it. *You* come up with another plan. I have work to do."

Ian left without another word, and Brock scowled his way through the rest of the morning, barricading himself behind the heavy wooden door to his father's ornate office. At twelve, he gave up the pretense of trying to work and began pacing. At twelve-thirty, he admitted pacing wasn't helping anything, either. At one, he pulled his Porsche onto the long, tree-lined stretch of road that led to his father's mansion.

There was a way around this, Brock knew there was. He simply hadn't thought of it yet. But he also knew pacing and scowling weren't helping matters. What he needed was to get Julia MacKenzie to trust him so that he could ease her into etiquette lessons again. He knew he wouldn't find his answer at the office, but he might find it if he could get to spend some time with her.

Not alone.

Particularly not alone in a bedroom.

Just time with her.

That way, she would see he wasn't an idiot or a monster, and would agree, at least, to have dinner with him again. Once she did, he would subtly teach her everything she needed to know, so that she wouldn't make any etiquette mistakes with Zack's grandparents. Which would give her the confidence she needed to be comfortable on their estate so she could easily show them what a good mother she was, and they'd realize there was no need to file for custody. Then she'd be content, provided for, and the Roberts family would have made up for their past mistakes.

And everybody would be happy.

In the house, Brock optimistically headed for the family room, hoping to join his father, Julia and Zack in some sort of game that might serve as the beginning for building trust. But as Brock walked through the downstairs of his family's home he discovered one little nuisance after another. Dirt smudges. Throw rugs angled in all directions. Knickknacks in the wrong places.

Eventually, he entered the pristine white living room and discovered the ultimate. He just barely stifled a gasp. There, with his little hand wrapped around the cord of a priceless Italian crystal lamp, was chubby, cherub-faced Zachary. Not only was the child just this side of filthy, but from the expression on his face, Brock could tell Zack was two seconds away from yanking the lamp off the table.

Brock lunged with a yelp and saved the lamp, but even as he snatched the tinkling crystal from the jaws of destruction, he saw the little boy's face pucker and wrinkle. Before Brock could stop that natural disaster, Zack burst into a screaming howl.

Julia scrambled into the room just in time to see Brock scare her son to tears. Two seconds after that, Frank hobbled in behind her, his hand clutching his thick black cane. "What the hell is going on here?" Frank barked angrily.

Great! Brock thought, frustrated. Not only had he alienated Julia by kissing her, but now he'd scared her child to tears and infuriated his father. "Nothing," Brock said, forcing a smile, as he realized there was only one way out of this. "I caught the lamp two seconds before it fell on Zack," he added, changing the story only slightly to make himself seem like a hero for saving Zack, rather than a villain for scaring Zack. So what if he'd actually saved the *lamp* from *Zack* and not the other way around? With the way this situation was panning out, Brock didn't have any choice but to alter the facts.

Even if no one else caught the nuance of change in the story, Zack did. He cast Brock a curious stare, then his lips curled upward into a superior grin, as if he realized Brock must not have had any choice but to save his bacon. Brock could tell from the question in his eyes that Zack wasn't quite sure why Brock had saved him. But from the cocky little grin, Brock could also see Zack was smart enough not to argue, even smart enough to press this situation to his advantage. He walked to Brock. "Up," he said, holding out his hands.

Brock's first thought was that Zack was a little too old to be carried, but when he saw the happy look on Julia's face, then the odd look of familial appreciation on his father's face, Brock bit the bullet. The way to the hearts of his father and Julia MacKenzie was obviously through the blue-eyed terror standing in front of him, and right now Brock needed to be on both of their good sides.

"Sure, sport," Brock said, reaching down to slide his hands under Zack's armpits to lift him. "Why don't we go into the family room and find a game to play?"

"Don't you think you should change out of that suit first?" Julia asked quietly, but there was an underlying skepticism in her voice that she couldn't quite hide.

"Nah," Brock said happily, shifting forty-pound Zack on his forearm to make them both more comfortable. "I'm fine."

Zack put his palms on Brock's cheeks and turned Brock's face to look at him. "Outside," he said simply.

"Outside?" Brock asked, puzzled.

"Zack loves to go outside," Frank explained. "But it's been a cold March and we haven't been able to let him in the yard."

"Outside," Zack repeated, again puckering Brock's cheeks as he forced Brock to look at him.

Brock glanced at Julia for approval. "It's not supposed to be that cold this afternoon. Can I take him outside?".

"I don't know," Julia hedged, and Brock knew that it wasn't skepticism he heard in her voice, but suspicion. She didn't trust him, not even with her child—*particularly* not with her child.

He supposed he didn't blame her. She had every reason in the world to have her qualms about him, and for a good mother that mistrust would certainly include her child. But Brock was home, right now, specifically at this minute, to get her to trust him again. Being good to Zack was the perfect and obvious avenue. He wasn't letting this chance get away.

"It'll be fun," Brock said. "Zack and I will have a good time. Just give me five minutes to change."

"No, that's okay," Julia said. Her tone shifted again, but in an odd way, a way Brock couldn't decipher quickly or easily. She reached for Zachary. "He can wait until tomorrow to go outside."

"No," Brock refused, holding on to Zack tightly. He knew he'd never get another opportunity as perfect as this one and he was keeping it. If it killed him—and going outside on a less than fifty-degree afternoon in late March with a forty-pound hellcat was definitely a healthy start toward killing him—Brock was taking this child outside.

"The kid's been cooped up for days. Let me do this. In fact, I'll just take Zack with me now, while I slip into jeans and grab an old sweater."

In his room, Brock slid Zachary to the floor. "Don't touch anything," he said firmly.

Zachary only grinned.

Brock stripped off his suit jacket. "You know, I only saved your butt this afternoon because I'm in more trouble with your mother than you could ever be."

Still grinning, Zachary watched Brock unbutton his shirt. "Outside?" he asked craftily.

"Yes, you're going outside. I'm going outside with you. We're both going outside because I think it will get us both in good with your mother."

At Zachary's confused look, Brock sighed.

"Well, if my luck holds, being outside will make you so tired, you'll go to sleep early tonight. Which will make your mother love you even more than she already does. But even better, if you go to bed early, I might get a few minutes alone with her."

After he said those words, Brock frowned. That didn't exactly come out in the way he'd intended it, yet, it didn't seem all that wrong, either.

Which was ridiculous. Sure, he found Zack's mother attractive. But he really didn't *want* to spend time with her. Not that spending time with her was exactly offensive. It was just that they were two different people who came from two different worlds. They had been accidentally thrust in the same world for a few weeks, so things were happening that wouldn't normally happen.

But Brock wasn't going to make a big deal of it. He was simply going to use Zachary so Julia would see he had good points and would like him again....

Good Lord, what had he done?

After the way he'd kissed her the night before, getting her to like him had an entirely different meaning today than it would have had yesterday. Instead of understanding Brock simply trying to reestablish trust, Julia was probably right this minute thinking that his being nice to Zachary was synonymous with courting her.

Brock slapped his forehead. Ian was right.

For a man who'd won so many academic awards, Brock could certainly be stupid sometimes.

Chapter Five

Brock returned from his outing with Zachary surprisingly refreshed and renewed, his head clear.

Calm and collected, he handed Zack to Mrs. Thomas, who took him into the kitchen for cookies and cocoa. Brock watched the little boy leaving with something akin to respect. Zachary might have babbled and walked through mud for the last forty-five minutes, but the kid certainly knew how to put life into perspective. Nothing was so drastic that you didn't have time to stop and smell the roses—or in Zack's case, stop and pat the mud cakes. After the short walk, with nothing more important on his mind than dodging puddles, Brock felt a hundred percent better.

As Brock thought the last, Jeffrey stepped out of the study corridor. "Mr. Roberts, a Harvy Dentenbaum called and requested that you call him back. Immediately."

"Thank you, Jeffrey," Brock said, then strode down the hall to the den. He placed the call to Compu-Soft, then took the seat behind the desk while he waited for his comptroller to come to the phone.

"What's up?" he asked when Harvy answered.

"I think I found the bid you're looking for."

Brock sat up. "What?"

"Well, there's a contract in one of our government bid lists that's coming around for the third time. I think no one's bid on it because it's too big for a little company and too small for a big company."

"But for a small company that's looking to expand, it's probably perfect."

"Precisely," Harvy agreed. "And since no one else wants it, Roberts Industries would probably be a shoo-in."

With a sigh, Brock sat back on his chair. "Thank you very much."

"Well, don't thank me yet. You still have to win the bid, and if you win the bid, the work's to begin the first week in September."

"The first week in September? My God, that means I'd have to have my building expansion started by at least the middle of May."

"That's how my figures pan out, too."

"But I don't even have an architect yet. Hell, I don't even have a loan yet!"

"Anything we can do?" Harvy asked carefully.

"No, just fax me that bid information. Roberts Industries' problems are Roberts Industries' problems. I've got to handle them here."

Brock replaced the receiver and collapsed in his father's chair. For some reason the deadlines in this mess just kept closing in on him. The way it looked, he had no choice but to go to plan B. And that was to liquidate his own assets to get the company's fanny out of debt. He still needed a power of attorney to get the loan, which meant he had to get Julia MacKenzie out of the house so she wouldn't overhear and take the news to town. But more than that, he needed his father healthy and eased back into his job before the work from the big contract came in.

Unfortunately, getting his father healthy was all wrapped up in fulfilling his bargain with Julia MacKenzie, and Brock knew that in spite of his time crunch he didn't have a choice. If he wanted his father healthy, he had to keep him happy, and that meant keeping Julia MacKenzie until Frank believed their debt to her was paid.

So, he was stuck. Caught in a catch-22. Stuck with keeping Julia MacKenzie so his father could get healthy. Because if his father wasn't healthy enough to handle this workload when the time came, Brock would really be stuck—stuck in Roberts Run permanently.

And that was something he simply couldn't tolerate.

Rising from the chair, Brock knew what he had to do. Ask Jeffrey to tell Julia that her presence was again required at dinner. Brock would do it himself, but he wasn't giving Julia the opportunity to refuse him. With Jeffrey as a middleman, Brock stood at least a fifty-fifty chance that she'd show up tonight.

When Julia arrived in the formal dining room that evening, dressed in a pretty peach dress from Angel's wardrobe, her hair pulled into a loose knot at the top of her head, Brock's jaw dropped. She looked gorgeous, captivating, exciting....

She looked like a woman trying to impress a man.

He swallowed hard. He'd been so caught up in working out the details for the contract bid, he'd forgotten he'd given her the wrong impression when he took Zachary outside. He got a gnawing feeling in the pit of his stomach, but before his awkward thoughts had a chance to fully gel, Brock involuntarily acknowledged that if she was trying to impress him she'd done a damned fine job.

The dress was a simple silk sheath. The scalloped neckline brought out the peach tones of her complexion. The delicate material clung to her curves. The skirt was long enough to be decent, but just short enough to tickle his imagination.

Quickly, in an act of self-preservation, he brought his eyes to her face, only to find himself examining her features with as much thoroughness as he had her body.

Julia's almond-shaped pale green eyes gave her an intriguing, almost mysterious air. Her high cheekbones and slim jaw accentuated her full pink lips. Her makeup was nothing more than a dab of mascara, some blush for her cheeks, and a light lip gloss. Brock decided that for Julia, makeup was unnecessary—what God hadn't given to her wasn't worth having. For a good sixty seconds, he was tempted, sorely tempted, to let her believe he'd taken Zack outside for all the wrong reasons—particularly since she seemed as interested as he was—and take advantage of this situation.

But the gentleman in him won out. He'd taken Zachary outside to win her good graces, but he needed to be in her good graces because of a business arrangement, not because of their mutual attraction. He genuinely believed it was not a good idea to follow this attraction. He knew one of them was going to get hurt—not him, since he'd be going into this with his eyes wide open—so he couldn't do this. No matter how tempted he was. No matter how much she seemed to want it.

"Julia," he said as she walked over to the table. He wasn't surprised that his voice quivered, then broke, merely with the speaking of her name. She'd literally taken his breath away, and he had to struggle to keep it. "Julia, I think I gave you the wrong idea."

"I beg your pardon," she said softly as she paused by her chair.

Realizing he'd been so busy staring at her he'd forgotten to seat her, Brock scrambled to attention. As he pulled her chair away from the table, he took advantage of the break in eye contact to say, "I think I gave you the wrong idea when I took Zack out this afternoon. I didn't do that because I like you. I mean, I like you," he amended hastily as he walked to his own seat. "And I think you're absolutely beautiful...breathtaking," he added because it was true and she deserved the compliment. "But even though I kissed you last night, I don't think it's a good idea for us to get involved."

"Involved?" she asked quietly.

"You know what I mean."

Her eyes narrowed and her nose wrinkled while she thought about that. "*I'm* the one who stopped that kiss last night," she said, confused. "Why would you think taking Zack outside would change my mind about getting involved?"

"What else am I supposed to think?" Brock said. Her answer baffled him to the point that he sounded every bit as confused as she did. "Look at the way you're dressed."

By this time Brock was seated, so—for better or for worse—he could see her face. He saw the expression of puzzlement that overcame her. He saw her think for a minute about what he'd said. Then he watched her face tremble for three seconds before she burst into uproarious laughter.

"I dressed this way to thank you," she said through her giggles.

"Thank me?"

"Well, yes," she said, calming now. "I know there's a reason you want me to wear your sister's clothes. I haven't figured it out yet, except that maybe you don't want to have to eat with a companion dressed like a street urchin. So when you were nice to Zack, even though it was killing you, I decided I'd do something nice for you in return." She paused, skewering him with a serious stare. "I didn't dress up for you. And I knew even before you kissed me that getting involved would be the stupidest thing you and I could do. I guess it's my turn to tell you not to take this the wrong way. I don't want to get involved with you, either, Brock. Probably more than you don't want to get involved with me."

It gave him no comfort that she didn't deny the attraction. If anything, that seemed to make his temper flare. Oh, she liked him well enough. But he was wrong about why she'd dressed up. She'd enjoyed his mistake, laughed at his misinterpretation, then just so the record wasn't clouded, she'd made damned sure he knew she'd rejected him first.

That rankled.

Jeffrey entered, offering appetizers.

Still angry, Brock deferred to Julia.

"Brock," she said slowly, sheepishly. "I don't know a thing about who gets what first, which fork you use, or where to put the food you choose from a serving dish. As long as we're eating together, I was thinking that maybe we should take advantage of this time to teach me some of this stuff so I don't embarrass myself in front of Zack's grandparents."

Brock only stared at her. Smiling slightly, she gazed at him with her slanted green eyes, looking something like a lost orange kitten. Sweet. Soft. Cuddly.

"Okay," he finally said. He had just gotten everything he wanted handed to him on a silver platter—by his own butler, no less—yet instead of being happy he felt cheated or tricked or something.

Damn it. He didn't know what he felt. He only knew he didn't like it . . . in spite of the fact that the opportunity to teach Julia was exactly what he wanted.

That rankled even more. Because he felt stupid, irrational, impulsive. And he hated those things.

"All right," he said, pushing his irritation aside and turning into his professional self, because it was his professional self that needed this bargain fulfilled. It was his professional self that was getting his father's company under control again. And his professional self that needed his father healthy enough to run the new company so Brock could go home. And his professional self that knew his father's recovery would be slowed to a crawl if Julia left before the Roberts family could make amends for their trouble with her. And his professional self that realized this burden fell to him because he was the only healthy Roberts living in this house right now. And his professional self that also recognized that if he taught her right and well, she'd leave. There'd be no reason for her to stay and no reason for his father to care if she left.

All those he understood. All that made perfect sense.

"I think you're right," Brock agreed as he faced Jeffrey and the serving tray. "It certainly couldn't hurt to help you...." He paused, choosing his words with care because he'd already proved that without skillful communications between himself and Julia, they did nothing but misinterpret each other. "Brush up on your social skills," he said at last, then smiled at her coolly, proficiently. With straightforward, proper lessons he could have her out of here in two weeks.

Thank God.

With everything out in the open about her need for tutoring, Julia handled the dinner with ease. She asked questions, hundreds of questions, and actually learned almost everything she needed to know about dining. Afraid that she'd consider herself schooled sufficiently and refuse to dine with him again—or refuse his companionship at all— Brock quickly considered his options, so that he wouldn't lose all the opportunities he needed to bring her along in the more delicate areas.

He pushed his chair away from the table slightly, and the sound it made scraping across the wooden floor echoed around them. Now that the meal was through there seemed to be nothing for them to talk about. As Brock realized the last, he knew he had his answer.

He cleared his throat. "Julia, have you thought about what you're going to talk about with Zack's grandparents when you meet them?"

She glanced at him sharply. "I've thought of nothing else. I assume we'll talk about Zack."

Looking into her melancholy eyes, Brock felt like he was drowning. She thought he was referring to the discussions about what would happen to Zack for the rest of his life, how he'd be raised, who'd have custody, when Brock was only referring to dinnertime conversation. Brock's was a careless question, a thoughtless question. But then again, he couldn't blame himself for a simple mistake because he and Julia didn't know each each other well enough to avoid sensitive topics.

A million unanswered questions existed between them. For instance, he couldn't understand why Zack's grandparents were pursuing Julia and Zack, and not Zack's father. Yet, Brock supposed the grandparents were the ones doing the pursuing since Zack's father proved himself disinterested enough to leave Julia alone and pregnant. Brock wondered how a man could desert a woman, especially a woman like Julia, but he also knew he couldn't touch that question with a ten-foot pole. Just like he had to stay away from the obvious now. He didn't have the time or the energy to get involved in her problems. He had enough of his own.

"No," he said, mentally berating himself for the thoughtless slip, even as he ignored its ramifications. "I didn't mean Zack," he clarified casually, trying to bring them back to neutral ground. "You can't talk about Zack twenty-four hours a day. I was thinking more along the lines of what you'd talk about in those times when you're trying to get to know each other."

"I've thought about it," she admitted reluctantly. "But I'm afraid I haven't come up with much of anything."

"Actually," Brock said, "I might be able to help you with that, too."

She glanced at him. "How?"

"Well, if you were to read *USA Today* and the *Wall Street Journal* every day, within a week, maybe ten days, you'd be completely current with world events."

"And?"

"And, every day, we could review what you've read, and I would teach you to be able to discuss world events in a non-inflammatory way."

Her lips tipped upward into an all-knowing smile. "In other words, I'm not allowed to have an opinion."

"Now, I didn't say that. The point that I was trying to make was that there are two ways to prove yourself to be knowledgeable. One is to show you know what's going on, another is to be able to objectively discuss the situation. No temper. No outrage. Just knowledge and reason. That'll prove you to be a capable person more quickly than having a son who doesn't break lamps."

She thought about that. "I suppose," she said, though she was loath to admit he was right. Only for Zack would she sell her right to have an opinion; for Zack she'd sew her lips closed if she had to. What Brock was saying didn't just make sense from the standpoint of coming across as intelligent because she was apprised of world events, but also from the standpoint of coming across as intelligent enough not to do battle over problems she couldn't solve. Which would, of course, make her look like a more capable caretaker.

It all made sense. Perfect sense. So much sense, Julia wondered why she hadn't thought of it, and just as quickly she wondered why Brock had. She glanced down at the beautiful peach silk dress, glanced over at his expectant expression.

Something was definitely going on here.

Chapter Six

The next morning Julia arrived at the breakfast table dressed in old, worn jeans and a rumpled sweatshirt. Her feet were bare, her hair sleep-tousled. She jogged to the double-door entrance, opened the doors wide, and burst inside like a sudden January wind. Unfortunately, when she saw Brock sitting at the head of the table looking like someone off the cover of *GQ*, she almost regretted her decision to use trickery to force him to admit he was up to something.

His shiny black hair had been combed into its usual neat style. But dressed in black trousers and a white cable-knit sweater over a black turtleneck, he looked better than he ever had in a suit and tie. And he'd looked pretty darned good in a suit and tie. Today, however, he looked scholarly, wonderful, worth every cent of the money his family had, and yet somehow casual, approachable.

Her bare toes hit the hardwood floor. She felt like an idiot.

Particularly when his face fell. "To what do I owe the honor of this getup?" he asked.

That was enough to get her dander up again. "What get-up?" she asked tartly.

He pulled her chair away from the table. "That," he said, indicating her torn jeans and rumpled sweatshirt. "You look like you slept in your clothes," he said, then caught a strand of her thick red hair between his fingers and feathered it away from her head. Before she could stop them, little ripples of pleasure danced down her spine. She ignored them.

"And this," he said disapprovingly, though his fingers lingered in her hair, twining through the strands as though examining their softness. "I've seen lions with neater manes."

"I've noticed you don't seem to mind touching my mane," she said, jerking away from him.

"And I seem to recall we've already closed that particular subject."

But they hadn't. Not really. At least, not as long as he continued to touch her, or to look at her the way he had last night as she climbed the steps to go to her room. He'd stood at the foot of the white spiral staircase, gazing up at her as if she were the most beautiful woman in the world. And it touched her because she could tell his admiration was genuine.

She knew he didn't want to be attracted to her any more than she wanted to be attracted to him, and that made the attraction all the more sincere, all the more potent, and all the more seductive. If it weren't for the fact that she knew his request for her to dress for dinner, his concise lessons during the meal last night, and his suggestion that she read the papers all combined to create some sort of trick, temptation might have overcome her common sense. She might have actually slipped back downstairs and shared the drink he'd offered her. But she hadn't because she knew something was wrong.

Yet, at this minute, the only thing that seemed to be wrong was Julia. She was dressed wrong, she was behaving wrong, and she couldn't seem to stop herself.

"I trust you slept well."

His comment caught her deep in thought and she cleared her throat to bring herself back to the present, trying to get herself to remember that the item at stake if she lost this chance to improve herself was nothing less than Zachary. Ashamed that she'd allowed her temper to convince her to risk this opportunity, Julia meekly said, "Yes. Yes, I did, Mr. Roberts."

He sat down, snapped his napkin open, and said, "Please don't call me Mr. Roberts. It makes me feel like my father."

"You're nothing like your father."

He lifted his juice glass, but stopped before he took a sip. He glanced at her. "I'm not sure if I should be insulted by that or not."

"I'm not sure if you should be insulted by it or not, either," she admitted faintly. "Look at me. Look what you've done to me. Your father never goaded me into dressing like this."

Brock did exactly as she asked. He looked at her. He looked at her hair, her face, her rumpled sweatshirt. His gaze lingered on her breasts, but no longer than it had lingered on her lips, her hair, her eyes. Nonetheless, by the time he was done looking at her, she felt thoroughly exposed. And vulnerable. Very vulnerable. Despite all the logic and common sense that told her she *shouldn't* want this man, she *did* want him. Julia knew that if he looked hard enough or long enough, one of these days he was going to see that.

"I'm not taking the credit for any of that."

"Well, you should," she said, angry now, though she was greatly relieved that her secret seemed to be safe for at least another day. "You forced me to dress like this."

Confused, his face puckered. "How in the hell could I possibly be responsible for that? If I remember correctly, not only have I encouraged proper dressing, but I've even offered Angel's wardrobe."

"That's exactly it. You did offer Angel's clothes. You offered *all* of Angel's clothes. You taught me everything I wanted to know last night at dinner, and now you're volunteering to talk me through conversation with the Whittakers."

He glared at her. "Let me get this straight. You're mad because I'm helping you?"

"I'm mad because you're helping me now, when two days ago you were trying to throw me out." Drawing a deep breath, she looked into his eyes. "I'm not stupid, Brock."

Nervous, he reached for the coffeepot. "I'm helping you. Honestly, generously helping you. And you—I presume from the way you're behaving—are throwing it all back in my face."

"I'm not throwing it back in your face, I'm calling you on it. I want to know why you're doing this."

With a long sigh, Brock made himself more comfortable in his chair. There was a part of him that wanted to admit that he knew the whole story about Ian's cheating and her losing her scholarship. He wanted to admit that he knew his father felt this to be their only chance to help her and he was taking it. He wanted to admit he needed her out of the house, so he was rushing things along, helping her as much as he could so she could leave quickly, as well as be compensated for Ian's mistake.

But he knew her pride couldn't take that. She'd have her bags packed and be on her way in twenty minutes. Then Brock would have to deal with an angry, disappointed father, a failing company and his own guilty conscience.

At the same time, he also knew that if he continued to plead generosity and benevolence, she'd never buy it. She was sure he had some ulterior motive—which he did—and unless he could come up with a convincing story, a reason seemingly sneaky enough, maybe even insulting enough, that she could accept it—he had no choice but to tell her the truth.

He sighed and opted for insulting her. He knew an insult wouldn't hurt her, if anything it would only prickle her spine and make her all the more determined to stay again. Which was exactly what he wanted—albeit for a limited period of time.

"I'm helping you because I think *you need help.* I know you think Zack's grandparents have called you up to Connecticut to discuss visitation rights, but it's my guess that they're planning to talk you into living there permanently."

As Brock said those words he knew they were true. He wasn't lying. He wasn't even insulting her as much as he was hitting her with the bare facts. He *was* helping her because she needed help. He might even be helping her for that reason more than to fulfill his own motives.

He sat a little straighter, felt some of his usual confidence return. "If you go there dressing poorly and acting afraid, they'll walk all over you. If you go there with a little poise and confidence, my guess is you'll make a much better deal. But no matter which way the chips fall, whether they wrestle Zachary away from you in a court of law and force you to live in Connecticut just to keep visitation rights, or whether they talk you into living with them, your life is about to change completely. Connecticut just might be your new home. You may never come back to Roberts Run."

The second the words were out of his mouth, a dead silence spread over them, as if both were struck dumb by the truth of what he'd just said. Julia stared at him, her light green eyes studying his, while he couldn't seem to tear his gaze away from her. They weren't thinking about her living with the Whittakers. What he had just said was tantamount to admitting that after this brief interlude they may never see each other again. It seemed to strike her as strangely as it struck him. He couldn't tell if her chest tightened, he couldn't tell if her breath lodged in her throat, as his did, but he could tell, from the expression in her eyes, that it affected her, even though she didn't want it to.

Without warning she slapped her napkin on the table and bounced from her seat. "Geez," she said, indignant. "Don't you think I haven't thought of all that?"

Recognizing her anger to be something of a defense mechanism for not dealing with the attraction between them, Brock calmly said, "No, actually, I didn't think you realized that."

"Well, I did. I have all along. Though Zack's grandparents made no bones about the fact that they want to file for custody, Moe's lawyer told me they have to prove incompetence before the judge would take Zack away from me because I'm Zack's biological mother. The lawyer says it would be much easier for them to try to talk *me* into living with them than to try to take Zack away from me."

"Makes sense," Brock agreed quietly. He leaned back in his chair, got comfortable. "So coming here, living here for the next few weeks, you're giving them exactly what they want. You're learning to live in their world."

"No," she said, then turned and looked him right in the eye. "Zack and I are here to try to get a little class."

"A little class?"

"A look," she said, pacing away from him again. "I'm assuming the Whittakers' biggest argument for trying to keep Zack and me in Connecticut will be that I can't give Zack everything that they can give him." She paused, rubbed her hands together as if trying to warm them. "But when you really get to the bottom line, the only things they can give him that I can't are superficial. I can give him love. I can teach him. And by being at your house right now I'm giving him class—which is the only thing, aside from money, that they could give him that I couldn't. When I first set my foot on those estate grounds, the Whittakers are going to see with one glance that their biggest argument is futile. That they might as well not even ask Zack and me to live with them because we don't need to."

Brock shook his head. "Julia, it almost sounds as if your being here actually defeats your purpose. If you refuse to live with them, they're going to have no choice but to file for custody."

"And that is their choice. But if they pursue custody, having lived here I'll put up a much better appearance in court. I'll have witnesses to the fact that I'm a good mother. And unless the Whittakers bribed the judge, I'll win because I'm Zack's natural mother."

Brow creased, Brock looked at her. "I thought you said you didn't know these people."

"I don't."

"Then what makes you think they'd bribe a judge?"

She shrugged. "It's an option rich people have that poor people don't. I don't know that they'd do it. I just know they're rich enough that they really can pull out all the stops to get what they want."

He thought about that a minute, then said, "Is that how you see me?"

"How I see you?" she asked, confused.

"Well, I'm rich. Do you think I'd pull out all the stops to get what I want?"

At that she laughed, a deep, rich, beautiful sound that echoed musically in the huge dining room. "Absolutely, without a doubt, I know that you'd pull out all the stops to get what you want."

He sat back in his chair again, crossing his arms over his chest. His lips pursed in his nearly vain attempt to keep them from bowing upward into a smile. Seconds ticked off the clock, and then finally he whispered, "I want you, and I haven't pulled out all the stops to get you, yet."

"That's because I come with a price," she said, and turned to face him. As if she didn't feel that was good

enough, powerful enough, she walked to the table and
leaned over it to face him. "I'm a mother. I come with a
three-year-old son born out of wedlock." As if to emphasize her next point, she picked up her butter knife. Gold-
plated, it gathered the light of a chandelier and winked at
both of them. "Somehow I don't think that matches your
image."

He was up and had her wrist in his fist before she even
realized he was going to stand. "Are you accusing me of
being a snob?" he asked, daring her to say the truth if that's
how she felt.

"I'm not accusing you of being a snob," she said, her
gaze locked with his, her breathing coming in short, scratchy
gasps because she was nervous. Not because she was afraid
of him, but because she *wasn't* afraid of him. He was much
taller than she was and so powerfully built his hug could
crush her. Yet instinctively she knew he'd never hurt her.
That knowledge made her last comment all the more insulting. He wouldn't hurt her, not physically, not emotionally.
Standing this close to him, knowing he would only be good
to her, she was quickly losing her perspective. Just as
quickly, his hold on her wrist changed from an imprison-
ment of sorts to a caress. The warm tingles that raced
through her blood as the slight touch of his fingers tempted
her to believe that the differences in their worlds meant
nothing. But Julia knew better. If money, social position, or
even good manners didn't matter, she wouldn't be fighting
David's parents right now.

She tried to pull away from him. "I've gotta go."

"No," he said, holding her exactly where she was.
"You're not leaving until we settle this."

"Okay, fine!" she said, indignant again. "Then let's get
back to the real issue. I know you're up to something. I
don't like being manipulated."

"I told you," he said, grabbing for the story that had
brought them to this place, but the story that was true

nonetheless and the story he decided to keep. "I'm helping you because I know you need help. Hell, you've even admitted it. One way or another, Julia, your life is about to become irrevocably linked to the lives of some very wealthy people. You can take my help or you can leave my help, but you most definitely need my help. So don't scream at me for offering it."

"I might need your help, but I don't need your charity," she said, yanking her wrist from his gentle grip. "And that's what this is."

"*This* is nothing more than an extension of the deal you had with my father."

She shook her head. "No, the deal I had with Frank was even. I helped him. He helped me. Your interference tipped the scales." She looked at him plaintively. "Don't you see, Brock? When this is all over with, I'll owe you."

"No, you won't," Brock insisted, as he inwardly damned her pride. He understood her pride. He understood that never having had anything, she felt everything was charity. But this wasn't. It was a business deal. "I swear to God you won't."

"You can say that now," Julia said, her eyes pleading with him. "But for the rest of your life you'll see me as that poor little waitress you helped...."

Eyes flashing fire, Brock said, "How dare you! How dare you make me sound so condescending again."

"Then why are you doing this?"

"All right. All right," he said, furious. "You want to know the truth? I'll give you the truth. I'm doing this because as it stands right now, we owe *you*. Your coming to work for us makes us owe you even more. My father feels guilty. My brother's ready to throw away the company's future, all to pay back this debt."

Her eyes hardened. "The scholarship."

"You know Ian cheated."

"Brock," she said, combing her fingers through her hair. "Half the town knows. Ian apologized about eight hundred times—mostly in the diner. He's offered me everything from money for college to a new car. And when he stopped, your father started. It took about two years of refusing gifts and money before they finally left me alone. And they've left me alone for the past five years. It's been so long, *I* even forgot about it. I just wish they had, too."

Brock looked at her as if she were crazy. "But why? Why won't you let my family make this up to you?"

"Because it's not my way. I forgive and forget." She combed her fingers through her hair again. "Don't you see?" she said, debating how honest to be because she knew sharing secrets bound people and she didn't want to be bound to Brock. She didn't want to be bound—indebted— to anybody. "I couldn't have used that scholarship, anyway. I was devastated after my mother died and was determined to raise my brother as well as if she'd been there for him."

Cautious, she glanced at Brock. "You can't do that and go to college. Besides, that was seven years ago. A million things have happened to me in those seven years that had nothing to do with that scholarship. No matter how it looks to you, Ian and even your father, the problems I have right now are *my* problems, not yours." She set the knife on the table. "So you're off the hook. Your entire family's off the hook. And I'm leaving."

He grabbed her wrist again. "You're not leaving. I'm not having my father think I insulted you or kicked you out. Particularly since I've been nothing but good to you. If you walk out that door, you'll ruin every chance I have of bringing Roberts Industries back to solvency, because there's no way in hell my father will sign a power of attorney if he's angry with me."

"I don't care about your power of attorney. I don't care if your company's insolvent." She said that, then paused, as if the meaning only then hit her. But she shook it off. "I don't take anybody's charity."

With that, she stormed out of the dining room and was about three steps into the foyer, ready to run to the stairs so she could go to her room to begin packing, when the words he said fully penetrated her conscious.

Had he really said Roberts Industries was insolvent?

Chapter Seven

Brock watched her go and even listened for the sounds of her feet pounding up the steps, though he didn't hear them. *The hell with her.* He was trying to help her and she kept throwing it back in his face. Unfortunately, though a proud and stubborn part of Brock wanted to feel that way, he also reminded himself that his father wanted to repay this debt; Ian wanted to repay this debt; even *Brock* himself wanted to repay their debt to her. Worse, if Frank found out Julia left because of an argument, he'd be angry first, then depressed, and then who knew how long it would take him to recover enough to be ready for his surgery.

As Brock thought the last, Julia came tiptoeing back to the dining room. She stood on the threshold, in the open double-door entrance, staring at him.

They both studied each other. A tangible electricity arched between them. They were oil and water, yet somehow, someway, they seemed to be bound to each other.

Slowly, reluctantly, Julia broke the spell. "You're going bankrupt?"

"The company is *floundering*," Brock said, emphasizing the less serious condition. "Our personal finances are fine, and the company itself is worth more than is owed to creditors."

"But there's a heck of a lot owed to creditors."

He conceded the last with a nod.

"I'm sorry."

Swearing under his breath, Brock turned away from her. That was it, the last straw. "You're a hell of a character, do you know that?"

Because he'd turned away from her, Julia moved behind him and peered around to glance at him. "Of course I know that."

Unconvinced, he shook his head. "No, you don't have a clue. Look at you. My family and our business aren't in half the trouble you are, and you won't accept help from me. Yet, my guess is you've come back in here to offer help, and you fully expect me to take it without question, without qualm."

He knew from the way her forehead wrinkled that she was thinking about that, and it confused her enough that she might actually be seeing his side.

"Now it's my turn to tell you I don't want *your* help." As those last words tumbled from his lips, Brock's mind stopped in midthought. By speaking too soon, he'd just made a colossal mistake. If he could get her involved in his family's crisis, then she'd have no reason not to accept his family's help. They'd be even.

"You're right," she said, stepping away from him. "I probably couldn't help you, anyway."

"Oh, you could," Brock said, thinking quickly, and coming up with a viable, obvious answer.

"How?" she scoffed.

He stared at her. "Don't you see that I need my father to recover as quickly as possible, so that he can get his surgery as quickly as possible and then recover from that, so that he's healthy enough to take over the company again once I have it solvent?''

"I understand that," she reluctantly admitted.

"Then you must not see that you and Zachary have been the force that's given him the motivation to get better. And if you leave, he's going to get depressed and his health will go downhill again."

He paused, waited for her to realize the truth of that, then added, "But now I can't ask you to stay because *I* absolutely refuse to owe *you*."

"Come on," she said, inching toward him again. "We're talking about losing hundreds of jobs here. If I can help, if I can do something to keep the company open so my friends stay employed, then I want to help."

"No," he said firmly. Nothing had ever turned so swiftly or so easily for him and he was savoring this. She'd had him by the ear for the last few days and now it was his turn. He'd never be able to make her squirm or even beg, but he could sure as hell spare the time to force her to make this her idea. "Just like you don't want my help, I don't want your help."

He saw in her eyes that she knew what he was doing. First they sparked, then they narrowed. "All right," she said, obviously harnessing her considerable anger. "All right. I'll stay here. I'll wear your sister's clothes and I'll read the *Wall Street Journal* every day. But you have to let me do more than sit here and keep your dad happy."

"That's all I need for you to do. I'm the corporate whiz, remember? I've already got plans in the works to liquidate some assets, pay off our debts and start some renovation projects that will put this company in the running for a very lucrative government contract."

She eyed him suspiciously. "I want to be in on more than just helping your dad get well. I want to do something at the plant."

"You don't need to."

"Then how do I know you're not pulling my leg? How do I know you haven't made this whole thing up to even the scales?"

He thought for a minute. "I could take you into the office and show you our accounts payable ledger."

She shook her head. "Anybody could show me a pile of old bills. I want to see you actually sell something."

"Sell something?"

"One of those assets you're planning to liquidate."

"Oh, okay." He nodded an agreement of sorts. "I'm selling land, so I could show you the deed, if you like."

"Then I need to hear how you're improving the company."

"You want me to keep a journal or just take notes?"

"How about filling me in on your progress every day when you come home from work?"

"Here's where I draw the line," he said, and walked back to his seat. "Look, I know you want proof that I'm not shamming you. I'm so well acquainted with your stubborn pride that I'm not even questioning that you'd want proof. Hell, I'm not even angry that you seem to be accusing me of chicanery. But now I have to draw the line, because my family needs some privacy."

Standing by his chair, he let several seconds tick off without saying anything.

"This is the deal, Julia, take it or leave it. You help me and I help you, but that's as far as it goes. I'm not sharing all the company's secrets." He paused, considered, then added, "This is an even deal, Julia."

"All right," she said, because she knew he was right. For as much as she wanted to help Roberts Industries, she also knew she needed Brock's help. It wouldn't be fair for her to try to pretend otherwise.

"That means you dress for dinner, and you read the papers so we can discuss them. I expect to hold up my end, but I can't do it unless you cooperate."

"Fine. I'll dress for dinner and read the papers, but only because this really is a good deal. But this is the last time I buckle under so easily. The next time we have an argument, don't think for one minute the pompous tyrant routine will work again."

"The pompous tyrant routine?" he gasped, incredulous that she could call anyone tyrannical after the way she not only manipulated him into admitting his family's troubles, but virtually made him beg just to let him help *her*.

"The pompous tyrant routine," she repeated. "I don't like it when you make declarations like 'this is the deal, take it or leave it.' From here on out we discuss things."

He strode in front of her, ready to jump into this argument with both feet, but the minute they were toe-to-toe—when he could clearly smell the fragrance of shampoo on her hair, and she could smell the crisp scent of his distinctive after-shave—another argument immediately came to mind. Both realized that the last time they were this close he kissed her.

Memories of that kiss flooded Brock.

Memories of that kiss tingled through Julia.

Brock felt himself being pulled forward.

Julia's feet ached to arch upward so she could stretch to meet him.

But when the thought completely registered that she wanted to kiss him, she shook her head as if to clear the smog from her brain.

"This is foolish," she said, moving away from him. "Why is it that every time I think we're about ready to come to blows, we end up almost kissing each other?"

"Or actually kissing each other," Brock reminded her as he took his seat again.

Julia ignored the warm starburst that poured over her as he said those delicious words. Instead, she started to pace. "Not only do we not get along, but we have conflicting temperaments. And, what makes this even funnier is that

I'm fighting for my life-style. Even if we were soulmates, which we aren't," she added with a significant look at Brock, "I don't want to live the way you live. If Zack's grandparents don't go after custody but only offer me the chance to live with them, to raise Zack with them, I don't want it. I love my life, poor though it is. I love my freedom, my neighbors, this community. You live in Boston, probably next door to a Kennedy. Even if you were the love of my life, I wouldn't want to live that way with you, any more than I want to live that way for Zack's grandparents."

Her candor would have made him laugh, if it hadn't insulted him. "Yeah, well, I happen to like my life, too. And I don't remember asking you to share it."

"Doesn't matter," Julia said, but she smiled. "You've just proven my point. We are incompatible. Which means that even though we're forced into this deal, it doesn't mean we're forced into following this attraction. And I don't think we should. Just don't turn pompous on me again, and we should be fine."

Brock only stared at her.

Her smile grew. "Good," she said, taking his silence as a backhanded agreement, and promptly left the room. Happy. Vindicated. He could see from the look on her face as she turned away from him that she thought this whole situation was very well under control.

Brock, on the other hand, collapsed against his chair. Not only had he just admitted to a perfect stranger that his family's company was on the verge of bankruptcy, but he wasn't entirely sure he agreed with her assessment of their attraction. Oh, he knew there was nothing permanent about it. If any two people were opposites and meant to live different lives, they were he and Julia. But the truth of the matter was, permanent or not, he had the damnedest urge to follow this attraction, if only to see where it would lead. Not only did he have more than a sneaking suspicion she'd be dynamite in bed, but he also realized no one, not a corporate lawyer, not his father, not his best competitor, ever got the kinds of deals out of him Julia had gotten. And he'd never felt more alive. Not even when he was saving Compu-Soft.

Unfortunately, the bigger concern was the fact that she knew his family's secret. She knew their trouble. In a moment of anger he'd blurted out the truth, and in a moment of desperation he'd taken advantage of it.

And Brock wasn't quite sure she could be trusted.

Chapter Eight

Knowing she was dressed and that he'd not be interrupting anything too personal, Brock went up to Julia's bedroom. Because it was Saturday, he wasn't going to the office. He knew Julia kept his father company every afternoon, but Brock decided he could handle that burden today and give her some real time off. Telling her that was a good enough excuse to seek private time with her again. He would wedge the real purposes for this discussion into the conversation as the opportunities arose.

He knocked once.

"Just a minute," she called out innocently, and Brock cringed, once again realizing she was expecting her caller to be someone else. He didn't feel guilty for interrupting her. He didn't even feel guilty for reopening their argument. What he hated were these sneak attacks, where she opened the door fully expecting to see his dad, or the maid, or the butler, and instead she found her nemesis, her adversary, her bête noire. Though why he should care, Brock wasn't sure. After all, she'd bested him at every turn so far. But he couldn't let her beat him this time. Not on this. His family's privacy was much too important.

When she finally granted him entry, Brock walked in uncomfortably. Sitting on the edge of the floral comforter on the bed, Zack was getting the Velcro strips of his shoe fastened. His round little foot was balanced against his mother's thigh. As Brock approached, Zachary looked up and smiled. "You take me outside?"

Instantly, as if by magic, all Brock's odd feelings vanished. He returned Zack's smile.

"Actually, Zack, that sounds like a terrific idea," Brock said and glanced out the window. The day was supposed to be somewhat warm for March, and the blue sky promised no rain. He turned to Julia. "There's an all-terrain vehicle in the garage. I was going to use it later this morning to check on the condition of the old farm I want to sell." He paused long enough to scoop Zack into his arms. "And I'd like to take Zack along."

Julia reached for Zack and set him on his feet. "He's too old to be carried all the time," she told Brock casually enough, but Brock could tell she was dead serious. So could Zack, who pouted but didn't argue. "But lucky for him that also means he's old enough to go gallivanting with you this morning."

"Hear that, kid?" Brock said, ruffling Zack's hair. "We get to ride the range together a little later on."

"Now," Zack said, grinning up at Brock.

"Well, I have to go see my lawyer first," Brock explained, or tried. Zack's plump cheeks sagged, his lips protruded, his eyes welled with tears. "Honestly, Zack," Brock said, resisting the urge to hoist Zack into his arms again. "When you get an appointment with a lawyer, you don't break it."

Zack didn't look impressed.

"I *have* to go," Brock insisted.

"But it's Saturday," Julia said.

"That's just the point," Brock said, turning his attention away from Zack, though he still kept a comforting hand on the little boy's head. "Since it's Saturday, no one will be out and about before ten and no one should see me sneak into Bill Morrison's office."

"You don't want anyone to see you going to your lawyer's?"

"No, I don't," Brock said. "I'm picking up the draft of a power of attorney Bill wrote for my dad to sign. But I'm also going to offer him the opportunity to buy the farm Zack and I will be visiting this morning, because he expressed an interest in the place when he drew up the papers for me to buy it. I'd prefer neither one of those transactions becomes common knowledge." He paused, sighing. Knowing there was no time like the present, he jumped in with both feet. "Look, Julia, I know you don't understand this, but I'm a real stickler for privacy. I shouldn't have blurted out my family's troubles to *you* this morning."

She looked at him curiously. "Why not?"

"Because they're not life-threatening, horrible disasters. They're a few minor difficulties. Difficulties that I'll be taking care of over the next few weeks. This time next year, my family won't remember the company touched horns with bankruptcy. But if even one word of that gets uttered in town, this problem will never be forgotten. And, more important, I can't risk my father hearing about any of this until he's well enough to hear about it. That also means I want him to hear it from me."

Still curious, she sat on the bed. She hooked her arms around her right knee and brought it up to her chest. "Let me get this straight. You don't want the town or your dad to know about your troubles, but you still want *me* to help you, right?"

"If you leave, my dad's recovery will be slow and difficult. Every week I have to wait for him to get better is a week I lose for putting the company back on its feet again. I honestly, genuinely, need you here to keep him happy and get him healthy."

"You just don't want me to tell anyone what you're do-ing."

"I should think that would go without saying."

"It did. So, why did you feel it necessary to come up here and say it?"

The note of insult and injury in her voice made Brock step back a pace. Even Zachary looked up at his mother, obvi-ously alerted to the possibility that a storm was brewing.

"You think I'm going to go running back to town with tales about your family, don't you."

"No," Brock immediately denied, then he grimaced. "I didn't think you were going to carry tales, but I also wanted to be sure that you understood the sensitivity of this prob-lem. Or at least that it would be disastrous for my father to find out before he's ready."

"I think we both know I realized that."

"Well, I also wanted to be sure you understood that se-rious though these problems are, they'll be forgotten if they're not advertised."

"And you think I'm going to advertise."

It was a statement, not a question, and though it should have made Brock feel guilty to be a gnat's eyelash away from accusing her, damn it, he wasn't. "I know you think I'm being unjust and unfair, but this is my house and my fam-ily. I protect what's mine." With that he turned and started walking toward the door. As he reached for the knob, he turned and faced them again. "Zack, I'll be back for you at around ten-thirty."

Julia was still furious when she knocked on Frank's door a few minutes later. Jeffrey answered, smiling, but when he saw the look on her face, he stepped aside without a word and went back to changing the linens on Frank's huge bed.

"Good morning, Frank," Julia said lightly, but through lips pursed so tightly they were turning purple.

"Hi, Srank," Zack said, peeking around Julia's knees to see Frank, who sat on the tapestry chair beside a round table. Behind him the bay window afforded a panoramic view of the beautiful woods that surrounded his property. No house or outbuilding destroyed the scenery. Only budding trees surrounded the neatly kept estate.

"Hello to my two favorite people," Frank happily greeted them as Julia set his breakfast tray on the table. Zack immediately crawled to the seat across from Frank, and, smiling, Frank watched him. Julia got a nudge of remorse for being borderline grouchy, particularly since she and Zack really did seem to make Frank so happy. But, dammit, she'd always known that. And she didn't even need to be paid to do it. If it wasn't so important to make this deal balanced, so both sides could walk away without feeling as if they'd accepted charity, she'd be here for nothing. It was the insinuation about her carrying tales to town that made her furious.

"He's dining with you this morning," Julia said, trying to create a chipper, silly mood and failing miserably. "I hope you don't mind."

"It's the joy of my day," Frank said while Julia opened the single serving of cereal. "But you don't seem all that happy about it."

"I like having Zack eat with you."

"Then what's wrong?"

"Nothing."

"Oh, you can't tell me nothing's wrong," Frank insisted good-naturedly. "I know better."

Jeffrey cleared his throat. "The bed is made, and if you like I could come back to finish the rest of the suite later this morning."

Frank glanced at Julia. "Yes, Jeffrey, I think that's a good idea."

"As you wish, sir," he said, then discreetly exited.

"All right, now that you've scared Jeffrey off, why don't you tell me what's bugging you?"

"Nothing's bugging me," Julia insisted.

Frank turned his attention to Zack. "What happened this morning, Zack? You wash your mother's blue jeans in the tub again?"

Zack giggled. "No."

"Did you flush her makeup down the commode?"

"No!" Zack said, still giggling.

"Did you . . ."

"He didn't do anything."

"Well, something happened, and since it's my house and you're my caretaker-companion, I have a right to know."

Suddenly, unexpectedly, Zack looked up at Frank and jubilantly announced, "Brock's taking me for a ride."

Frank glanced at Zack, then at Julia. "Oh, he is, is he?"

"Yeah."

"And when was this decided?" Frank asked, but he looked at Julia.

Julia sighed. "This morning. Brock told me he was taking the all-terrain vehicle out and asked if he could take Zack along."

"So, you've already made contact this morning," Frank stated with an all-knowing smile. "And he's already made you mad."

"He says the stupidest things, Frank."

"Well, of course he does. He went to the kind of college most of us can only dream about and runs a company three times the size of mine. To do all that, Ian and I figure Brock's got to have a different brain or something. Most of us aren't on his wavelength."

"Oh, I'm on his wavelength, all right."

"I'll bet the stupid thing he said wasn't really stupid as much as it was insulting."

"He thinks I'm going to carry tales when I leave your house."

Frank sighed. "Stop pacing, Julia. Take a seat on the bed or something and let me explain a few things to you."

"You can't explain away the fact that your son is an idiot."

"How about if I tell you he has good reason to be an idiot."

"No one has good reason . . ."

"Uh-uh-uh. Now it looks like you're jumping to conclusions."

"All right. What good reason does your son have for accusing me of carrying tales when he has no idea of whether I would or not?"

"It's not you, Julia. It's the town. Brock has an innate dislike for living in this town."

"But why? And what does that have to do with me?"

"Well, the answer to both questions is the same. All through high school Brock was something like public property. He was outscoring his peers in aptitude tests and getting scholarship invitations like no one before him ever had. Did you know he didn't have to complete his senior year?"

Julia shook her head.

"Well, he didn't."

"That's peachy."

"No, it wasn't. He lost what is for most teenagers the most important year of their lives, gave it up because he couldn't take the pressure. Teachers treated him differently. His classmates treated him differently. Everybody acted as if he was somehow going to put them—and this town—on the map or something. When all he was was a genius."

"Poor kid."

"Now, Julia, it wasn't easy. His life has never been easy. And, in fact, things got worse once he graduated. Everybody always seems to know what he's doing. I don't know where they get their information. I don't know *how* they get their information. The point is, somebody *always* gets the information. Not everything, but enough. Just enough to make him feel that his life isn't his own." He paused, considered, then said, "Let me ask you something. Do you know how much Brock earns each year?"

Julia automatically recited the figure she'd heard through gossip, and immediately realized what Frank said was true.

"Ah, I can see from the expression on your face you're starting to sympathize."

"Not sympathize. Understand, maybe, but not sympathize."

"Understanding is good enough. Brock could use some understanding. Maybe he could even stand not to have to be the one everybody depends on all the time."

Even as he said those words, Julia felt uncomfortable. Frank had no idea how much everybody was depending on Brock right now because he had no idea that his company was in financial trouble.

"Your breakfast is getting cold," Julia said, choosing to ignore his final remarks.

Frank scowled. "Oatmeal and sugar. Now it's my turn to say 'peachy.'"

"It's only for a couple more weeks," Julia said sympathetically.

Frank looked at her. "It's the rest of my life, Julia. If I want to stay healthy." Suddenly, he glanced up at Julia. "What time is Brock coming by for Zack?"

"Ten-thirty."

"I'm going to shower after I eat this," he said, referring to oatmeal. "Then I'd like to play cards this morning."

"Okay," Julia said easily. "I'll have Jeffrey watch Zack in the family—"

"No," Frank casually refused. "Let him play up here with us. It won't hurt Brock to come up here to get him."

Chapter Nine

When Brock arrived home from his appointment, Jeffrey immediately directed him to his father's room where he found Frank and Julia deeply immersed in a game of rummy, while Zack rolled a plastic truck on the hardwood floor.

"Come in. Come in. We could use another player," his father boomed when Brock opened the door.

"Sorry, Dad, I promised Zack I'd take him out on the all-terrain vehicle this morning," Brock said, but he caught the odd look Julia gave his father, as if to say Frank already knew that.

"Oh," Frank said, arranging his cards. "Where are you going?"

"To the farm," Brock said, his tone cautious because Julia was still giving his father a confused look. "I decided to sell the old Connor place."

Frank glanced up sharply. "But you love that place."

"I did," Brock conceded with a nod.

"So why sell it?"

Brock cleared his throat. "Because the property value's not going up and the taxes are a drain. I can put that money to better use investing it." He shrugged carelessly. "It's a simple investment decision."

"Brock, I have a little extra money in my savings if you need . . ."

"Dad, I don't need money. I'm just playing with my investment," Brock said, then took a seat on the edge of the bed to keep from pacing because the lie made him nervous. "You're the one who taught me to treat investing as a game. I've just decided on a new strategy."

Looking at his cards, Frank quietly said, "A foolish strategy. That property's bound to be worth three times as much a few years from now. Besides, I thought we'd agreed that you would settle there someday. At least make the farm a summer home."

"I don't want a summer home."

"Or is it that you don't care to live near to your family?"

"Dad, this isn't a matter that's open for discussion," Brock said honestly. "It was an investment decision, plain and simple. It's my money, my investment. The decision is made and final."

"I see."

"If he's so eager for money," Julia said innocently enough, though Brock knew she was getting him out of this conversation in a way only Julia could manage, "we could always up the ante on the rummy, and let him try his luck here at the game table."

"To earn the money from you?" Frank asked, then he laughed. "Julia, you're a pistol. If you think I'm so senile that I don't realize you'd up the ante on the rummy so you could beat the tar out of both of us, you're crazy."

She raised her hands helplessly. "It was worth a shot."

"Yeah, well, I caught you," he said, then pushed his chair away from the table. "Besides, I'm suddenly tired."

"Oh," Julia said, bouncing from her seat. "Zack and I will leave, then."

"Zack's going out with Brock, remember?" Frank said, huffing as he lifted himself out of his chair. "So you're going to have to entertain yourself for the rest of this morning." He paused, looked at Brock, then at Julia, and said, "You know, it really is silly for Julia to stay here this morning when I feel a long nap coming on."

"You're not taking a long nap," Julia protested. "You go for a walk right before lunch."

"Jeffrey will take me," Frank said. "In fact, he'll get my lunch. I want you to go along with Brock and Zack."

"But—" Julia stammered, not thinking of a valid reason.

"But—" Brock said, "I can't put three on the all-terrain vehicle."

"You have to drive the pickup over to the Connor place because you can't take the all-terrain vehicle on the road. So there's plenty of room for Julia in the truck. I'm not saying Julia should ride the ATV with you, she should just get out of the house for a while so she can get some air and I can get some peace."

There was an underlying tone of exhaustion in his voice that had Brock casting a sidelong glance at Julia. She smiled helplessly, and though Brock thought he'd steeled himself against the effects of that smile, his heart froze for a good three seconds... until he realized she wasn't smiling at him because she liked him, but to get the point across that she felt they should do Frank's bidding.

"Okay, Dad," Brock said, rising from the corner of the bed on which he sat. "That sounds like fun."

"Take a picnic lunch," Frank instructed as he slowly made his way to an easy chair and picked up his television remote. "Stay out all afternoon."

"Sure," Julia agreed, edging toward the door. "Fine."

* * *

"On a scale of one to ten, how upset did you think he was?"

Julia glanced at Brock. Zack was running around a tree, for God knew what reason. Brock and Julia sat on a blanket—Julia packing away the last of their picnic; Brock, dressed in threadbare jeans and a paint-splattered sweatshirt, deep in thought. As she cleared their food and stashed their used picnic utensils, Julia had covertly watched him, knowing he was so lost in his contemplation that he'd never even notice.

She'd always believed that it was his sophistication, his mode of dress, his manners, the beautiful way he spoke, that gave her the giddy bubble in the pit of her stomach when he was around. But today, seeing him dressed like a construction worker, noting that his muscled body gave meaning and life to an otherwise unattractive outfit, Julia was coming to see that her attraction to him had inched beyond superficialities. Any woman who could think a man looked completely sexy and totally appealing in a paint-splattered sweatshirt was definitely finding the personality more appealing than the looks.

Which shouldn't surprise her. No matter how hard she tried to fight it, she was really beginning to like him. And why not? He was good to his father, terrific with Zack, and good to her, too. He didn't have to be nice to her. Even though he'd read her situation very well, understood it better than she did sometimes, there was no law that said he was duty-bound to step in and take over for his father. Yet, he had. He was very good to his father. Very protective.

"How upset do I think your father was over your selling the Connor place?" Julia asked, and Brock nodded. "You know him better than I do."

Smiling ruefully, Brock said, "I was just about to tell you the same thing."

"Come on," Julia chided. "You're his son. You've been his son for more than thirty years. I've been his caretaker for less than thirty days. You know him better."

"I might have been his son for more than thirty years, but I've been away for twelve. Thirteen, actually. We have Thanksgiving, Christmas and Easter together." He shrugged. "Sometimes I feel like I don't know him at all."

"He seems to know you very well," Julia said, seeking only to balance the conversation, and not realizing she'd given away the fact that she and Frank had discussed Brock.

"Oh, really," Brock said, smiling. "And just what did my father tell you about me?"

The expression on his face was so blatantly flirtatious, Julia almost gave in to temptation. Almost. Brock might be an attractive man, and a good man, but their worlds didn't mesh. She didn't have to go through a second heartache to confirm a relationship between them wouldn't work. But this time, because she knew she genuinely liked him, the regret of succumbing to that logic was deeper, stronger, than it had been every other time she talked herself out of surrendering to the moment with him.

Knowing she couldn't take the obvious roads, she couldn't tempt or tease, or dangle the truth to make him beg for information until both were laughing from the game of it, Julia only said, "He told me that you're a genius."

Putting her attention back on gathering their leftovers, she added, "He's very proud of you, of what you've done, all you've been through."

"Yes, well, what my father fails to realize is that once I left Roberts Run my struggles weren't all that bad."

"Self-made," Julia said, pondering. "And telling me it was easy. I'm impressed."

"Don't be. After the trials and tribulations I had here, even pulling a company from the jaws of its creditors was a cakewalk."

Confused, Julia considered that. She thought of her little town, of the regulars at the diner who left her generous tips the first week of the month because they knew her rent was due. She thought of the baby shower they'd had for her. How two of her friends had even gone together to buy her a new crib and mattress. She thought of the safety of her streets. The easy way of life. The friends. The camaraderie. She couldn't imagine that these people, nosy though they sometimes could be, would have done something so terrible as to make a very clear-thinking man like Brock dislike them so much. She knew it had to be more than their constant curiosity about his life. Once a person passed the age of twenty-two they knew the foolishness of worrying about the opinions of others. So something must have happened to make him so...so...bitter? Cynical?

Cynical. That was it. Brock was cynical.

Curiosity overwhelmed her and she peeked at him. "What happened to you here in Roberts Run that was so terrible?"

He rose. "Nothing," he said, and began walking toward Zack. "Come on, cowboy. We'll take one last tour of the Ponderosa and then we'll head back to the main ranch."

Knowing Brock and Zack were about to bounce their way around all one hundred acres of this overgrown property again, Julia bounded to her feet. "Be careful!" she said, scrambling over to Zack so she could stretch a knit cap over his head. She turned to Brock. "And don't let Little Joe pull this off halfway around the south pasture, either."

"Yes, ma'am," Brock said, giving her a salute. Then he sobered. "Will you be okay for the fifteen minutes we're gone?"

His look was so intensely concerned that she felt herself blush. He cared about her, too. She'd suspected it before, but now she knew. They were an odd pair, thrown together by circumstance, and soon to be torn apart by the same circumstance. It would be foolish, no matter how inviting his lips, no matter how sincere his eyes, no matter how much she longed to touch the silky locks of shiny black hair that fell to his forehead, to fall in love with someone she couldn't have.

Folding her tempted hands together to quiet them, she shrugged. "Yeah. Sure." She grinned sheepishly. "Actually, I'll probably enjoy the quiet."

Before Julia realized what Brock was about to do, he bent and placed a quick, chaste kiss on her lips. "Thanks," he said, and, hoisting Zack into his arms, he turned away from her and began striding toward the ATV.

"For what?" Julia called after him, absently touching her fingertips to her startled lips. Her heart was beating a million miles a second. Her body had been stunned into immobility. Only one tiny corner of her brain remained functioning, and that part had, luckily, kept control.

He turned, faced her with a smile. "For listening."

"But you never said anything," she said, confused. "So I didn't listen."

"In your own way you listen. You pick up on the things I don't say."

"Oh, that makes sense," Julia mumbled, but he had turned away from her and didn't hear.

Chapter Ten

After dinner the following Saturday night, Brock pushed his chair away from the table and walked behind Julia to pull hers out for her.

"Since you've done so well over the past week, and since it's Saturday and both of us can sleep in tomorrow, we're going to take your lessons one step further tonight."

Though he never touched her, Julia felt Brock's hands at the back of her chair. She felt the magnetism of his body as he stood behind her. A constant electric current seemed to arch between them, but when he was this close the sensation was so intense it nearly took her breath away, and her mind automatically jumped to the last time he'd kissed her. An entire week had gone by since that kiss, but there were times her lips still tingled from the memory. The passionate kiss was one thing, something she could relegate to pure attraction. But that one short, chaste kiss spoke volumes, even though she'd tried not to pay any attention.

She cleared her throat. "We are?"

"Yes," he said, holding out a hand to help her stand. "Tonight, we're going to have brandy in the living room while we discuss world events."

"I'd rather have a glass of beer out on the patio," she said, trying to lighten the mood to get her mind away from places it shouldn't be. Then, answering his scowl of displeasure, she added, "But since I know that end of it's probably non-negotiable, I'd like to ask that we save the newspaper conversation for breakfast."

"Is there something on your mind that you'd like to talk about?"

Julia took a second to compose herself by drawing a deep breath. She knew how Brock felt about his privacy, but a deal was a deal, and, like it or not, he was keeping this one. "No, but I think it's time you start holding up your end of the bargain by telling me how things are going with your problems at the company."

Placing her hand in the crook of his elbow, Brock considered that. But not for long. From the expression on his face, Julia could see that he wanted to protest, but quickly realized if he didn't tell her he would be reneging on his end of the deal. They had a shaky peace at best, partially because they were so darned attracted to each other, and partially because their ideas about propriety were so far apart. He had to tell her something or their pact was over. It was that simple.

"Truthfully, Julia, though I have some irons in the fire, there's not much to tell yet," Brock said, and Julia breathed a silent sigh of relief that she wasn't going to have to argue with him. "Selling the Connor place will take care of most of the overdue bills," he said as he led her to the door. "But I still have to get my dad to sign a power of attorney before he goes into surgery. That's only common sense. I'm not going to tell him I *need* the power of attorney, only that it's wise to have it on hand. But, realistically, once I get that power of attorney I can do whatever needs to be done with the business, including initiating the proceedings for the renovation loans if I want, and I won't have to involve him."

"Do you really think that's fair?" Julia asked as they walked across the white ceramic floor of the foyer, her black satin pumps marking each of their footsteps. Tonight she wore a multicolored knee-length sequin dress. Rather than pull her hair into a chignon or bun, she'd curled it with electric curlers and let it fall in soft, fluffy curves. Surprisingly enough, she felt almost normal. After a few weeks of living in this house, and a little more than a week of wearing good clothes and eating in the formal dining room, she was growing ridiculously comfortable. Except for that one kiss. That chaste kiss that hinted that Brock was feeling things stronger than lust, more potent than desire. He actually liked her.

"Julia, I honestly don't believe my father's well enough to hear about all this yet," Brock said as escorted her to the sofa, then walked to a discreet bar in the back of the room, which was to the right of the light stone fireplace. Someone had started a fire, which provided a background hum and dressed the usually bright white room in muted yellow light. Brock didn't make a move to turn on any of the lamps, and though the room was a little too cozy, a little too intimate, for their purposes, neither did Julia.

"We're going to be drinking brandy," he instructed, pulling a bottle from the shelves below him. "But we're going to start with peach-flavored brandy because it's more pleasant-tasting. We'll work our way up to regular brandy as you grow accustomed to its bite."

"If brandy tastes so bad, why are we drinking it at all?"

"Because if you have to drink something, ask for brandy, and then you can sip it all night and no one will wonder why."

"Really?"

"Yes, really. Brandy's a sipping drink," he said, handing her a snifter. "So you get one glass, and you sip it all night. You'll fit in without having to worry about getting drunk.''

She conceded the wisdom of that with a nod. "Makes a weird kind of sense."

"Yes, it does. Now, put just the tiniest drop on your tongue, but be prepared. It'll burn."

"Why do people drink this stuff?" she asked, grimacing at the glass even though she'd yet to taste the brandy.

"Because it really does taste good after a few sips," he said, casually draping his arm across the back of the couch after he took the seat beside her.

Though he meant nothing by the simple gesture, Julia's nervous system went on red alert.

"Besides . . . that bite also makes you warm, keeps you from being nervous. Trust me, it's exactly what you'll need."

"All right," she said, casting him a skeptical glance, but realizing that if he was right, she needed a glass of brandy now every bit as much as she'd need it to face the Whittakers. "I'm taking your word on this."

He smiled his encouragement, and she daintily placed the glass to her lips and carefully, ever so carefully, laid a drop on her tongue.

She blinked. "I see what you mean."

"Eventually," Brock said, "once you get comfortable with the glass and the liquor, you'll let it sit on your tongue long enough to savor the warmth and the flavor."

"I doubt that."

"Humm. We'll see," he said, then brought his own glass to his lips and took an adequate sip. Mesmerized, Julia watched him enjoy the liquid and saw the subtle expression of contentment that lit his face before he actually swallowed it.

"While we talk, you play with that. Don't worry about what's right and wrong, just try to get used to the taste. All right?"

Quickly pulling her gaze away from his face, Julia nodded.

Brock set his glass on the coffee table, then sat back on
the couch again, getting comfortable. Toying with her glass,
Julia covertly studied him and decided black was definitely
his color. She supposed that's why he wore it so often. The
deep hue of his suit highlighted his dark eyes and beautiful,
silky-looking black hair. Yet, even with his swarthy hair and
eyes, he didn't look imposing or sinister. As always, he
looked incredibly natural, relaxed. Having grown accustomed to wearing formal clothes, Julia could now understand how he looked so casual in his all the time. But still,
his general demeanor went beyond comfortable. He gave a
twist of sex appeal to elegance that was nearly irresistible.
He made refinement sensual, sexy, almost arousing.

"So, anything else you want to talk about?" he asked
blithely.

"Huh?"

He smiled.

Little bursts of attraction exploded in Julia's chest.

"I asked if there was anything else you want to talk
about?"

"Uh, no," Julia admitted quietly. "I suppose if you really want to we could discuss the newspapers tonight."

Her voice trailed off in a plaintive way that echoed
Brock's feelings. They were attracted to each other, but
fighting it like the devil because it was pointless; and it was
driving both of them crazy. Yet, he frequently dated women
that he had no intention of marrying but with whom he
shared common interests. In Boston, no one thought that
odd or unusual. But in Roberts Run it was almost a crime.
Still, he'd chosen to reject Roberts Run rules of protocol
long ago, and, whether she knew it or not, Julia was reject-
ing them as well. Maybe this was another lesson she needed
to learn—here, from him—before she set off for the real
world.

Without another thought, he reached for Julia's brandy snifter, took it from her hands, and set it on the coffee table beside his. Before she had a chance to consider what he was doing, or to react, he slipped his hand behind her neck, under her thick, luxurious bounty of hair, pulled her forward and covered her mouth with his own.

Nothing could have prepared him for the fact that she didn't merely respond to him, she appeared to have been as starved for this kiss as he. Once over the initial confusion, her mouth opened and she met him hungrily, eagerly, her soft body molding into the contours of his as they both slid down on the couch. Her fingers made thin, tingling trails tunneling into his hair. The stiff sequins of her dress were cool against his hand, but the skin of her arms was soft, warm, pliant. And her hair felt like satin, sleek and sensual.

Suddenly, everything Brock knew, or thought he knew, about himself, about women, about himself with women, became meaningless. His control was slipping, and he was still lucid enough to know that once it was gone, he'd never get it back. But, worse, he didn't care. There was something so compelling about this woman and this moment that instinct superseded logic and yet somehow managed to feel perfectly right.

Julia felt like she was drowning. If there was such a thing as desperate passion, she'd just found it, or entered it. In spite of the fact that she knew this was wrong, she couldn't help herself. Not because she was simple or greedy, but because she had been pulled into something she didn't understand, but something that somehow made sense in her completely unstable world. She couldn't say how it made sense or why, only that it did. Only that there was a security and comfort that in some way joined with need and desire to create an instinct so passionate and so pure she was incapable of resisting it.

The smooth softness of his clean-shaven cheek called for her touch, his mouth begged for hers. It had never been like this with David, and though she didn't mentally make the comparison, it was there. She knew that might have been because David and Brock were so different. Where David was carefree and unfettered, Brock was controlled, serious. She'd loved David with all her heart and soul, but she'd never felt he needed her. Brock needed her. She could feel it.

Something troubled him, and it was here in Roberts Run. Yet he'd come home, stepped into his father's shoes and taken over the factory, the most public position in their little town, without hesitation and without qualm. Whatever his demon, he faced it every day.

She could comfort him in this space of time that he was home; and they might actually fall in love. But if they did, would she be willing to give up everything she was fighting Zack's grandparents to keep? Or would Brock be willing to stay in this town he seemed to dislike so much?

The answer to both questions was such a quick and resounding no, that Julia felt herself pulling up short. With one final taste of his mouth to keep her memories rich and alive and a sense of regret so deep and so tangible she felt a physical pain, Julia pulled away from him.

She knew in her heart that the pain she was feeling right now, intense though it was, was nothing compared to what she'd feel the day he told her he was going back to Boston—without her. She'd deal with this hurt now because the one that would come later would be a hundred times as strong.

And she'd do anything, absolutely anything, to protect herself from that anguish.

Chapter Eleven

Frank didn't question Julia's request to have Sunday off, and Julia never asked Brock's permission to forgo Monday morning's breakfast. She simply didn't show up. The situation was too confusing. She knew there could never be a relationship between her and Brock. They led two different kinds of life-styles. She was fighting for hers. He'd already fought his battles and won. Neither one of them intended to give a fraction of an inch. Yet every time he came near her, every time he touched her, they both forgot all that. Distance, keeping away from each other, was the best alternative. And it worked all weekend.

But, after having taken Frank to his doctor's appointment and receiving the news that his surgery had been scheduled for the following week, Julia stood in the lobby of Roberts Industries. Holding Zack's hand and staring at the building directory, she contemplated the wisdom of meeting Brock in such a public place. She was fairly certain he wouldn't kiss her or hug her or even touch her in front of witnesses, which made this safe. But for every bit as safe as it was, providing he acted with decorum, it was equally unsafe if he acted out of instinct.

In the end, Nadine Pierson, the receptionist, made Julia's decision for her when she rose from her seat and asked, "May I help you with something, Julia?"

Julia licked her suddenly dry lips. "Yes, I'm here to see Mr. Roberts...Brock," she clarified, remembering Ian also worked here.

"I'll announce you," Nadine said, pulling her telephone receiver from its cradle. "Mary, would you please tell Mr. Roberts that Julia MacKenzie is here to see him."

There was a pause, and Zack began to squirm.

"Remember, Zack," Julia whispered down to her son. "If you're good, we'll stop at Moe's for pie."

Zack stilled immediately.

Nadine returned the receiver. "Mr. Roberts asked that you come right up."

"Thank you."

Julia led Zack to the narrow stairway, a reminder that this factory had been built so many years ago that it desperately needed remodeling. It was also a reminder of her real mission. That stopped the quaking in her knees as she climbed the steps and even kept her calm while waiting in Brock's secretary's office. But when he stepped through the oak door, looking formal and businesslike in his dark blue suit and his blue tie, his hair sleek and sophisticated, his expression reflecting the fact that he'd been deep in thought, Julia felt her heart flip-flop. He attracted her dressed in jeans and a sweatshirt, dressed in a suit, even when he bossily directed her to watch her posture. She couldn't look at him without feeling an emotion so deep it made her tingle.

And it was pointless, worthless, fruitless, because they simply were not meant for each other. No matter how many times he kissed her, no matter how much she liked it, they were opposites. People with opposing goals. People who should be smart enough to keep their wits about them....

But damn, he looked good, and part of her was getting awfully tired of fighting this because it just plain didn't seem fair to want somebody so much when you couldn't have him.

Pushing those thoughts right out of her head, Julia drew a quiet breath. "Hi," she managed to say self-consciously.

"Good afternoon, Julia," Brock said with a nod. "Zack," he added more exuberantly as he bent and lifted Zack off the ground and into his arms. After searching out some coins from his pocket, he handed them to his secretary. "Mary, run down to the vending machines and grab a snack for our little friend."

"Sure, Mr. Roberts," Mary said, obviously surprised by his order.

But Julia wasn't surprised. First, she figured Brock didn't want any witnesses in case they decided to do battle, as they sometimes did. Second, he spoiled Zack pitifully. And third, the people of this town didn't know Brock the way Julia did, and she suspected they never would.

He directed her into his office—Frank's office—and while she took a seat on one of the chairs across from his desk, Brock settled Zack on his lap. Perfectly content, Zack sat and stared directly at Brock's face.

"I missed you at breakfast."

"I slept in," she said, lying because it was easier than telling the truth, which would lead to an argument. "I'm here because Jeffrey and I took your dad to the doctor this morning."

That got his attention. "And?"

"And the pneumonia's gone. Completely. Dr. Brown's scheduled him for angioplasty next week. He doesn't want to waste time and risk your dad getting sick again. So he's decided to do angioplasty rather than bypass surgery."

"And it's next week?"

"Yes, next week. Brock, you're going to have to get that power of attorney signed within the next couple of days."

"Not necessarily," Brock said, leaning back in his chair as Zack sat forward and began rearranging things on Brock's desk. A thick marker quickly caught his attention.

Unexpectedly, Zack glanced up at Brock. "Color?"

"Sure, sport," Brock said, and began looking through the papers and files on his desk until he found a tablet. He ripped off the first several pages which contained writing of some sort, then rose from his chair and walked Zack to a low table in front of a couch and chair. "Knock yourself out."

As he walked back to his seat behind the desk, he said, "I was thinking about this last night and realized that if I liquidated most of *my* personal assets, some stocks and bonds, on top of selling the Connor place, we might not need to drag my father into this at all."

Julia gasped. "Brock, you can't do that."

He shrugged. "Why not?"

She answered his question with a question. "Why? Why sell your own things when you've already told me the family has plenty of money to cover these debts?"

"Because after I pay the debts, I'll still need a loan. My dad doesn't have enough money to pay the debts and cover the renovations."

"And you do?" Julia asked incredulously.

He smiled wickedly. "I guess we'll find that out once I start selling things."

"Why don't you just get a loan from the bank?"

"Because I'm stuck," he said tiredly, obviously realizing she'd argue this point to the death with him unless he came clean. "I can't tell my father how much trouble the company's in a few days before he goes into surgery. But I also won't feel comfortable liquidating my family's assets without my father's permission, and that's exactly what I'd have to do. Even if I got a power of attorney signed, I'd be selling his things without telling him, because he won't know that's why I got the power of attorney signed. Besides, I'll just look at this as an investment. Once I get through with renovations, this factory will be a gold mine again. Why drag my father through the embarrassment of getting a loan when we don't have to?''

Though his answer made perfect sense, it didn't really make any sense. If the overdue bills were paid, and Brock sought a loan only for the factory improvements, the bank wouldn't look at this loan as a rescue mission, but as a renovation project. It might take several weeks to get all the papers processed, but getting a loan wasn't all that big of a deal. Brock's saving the company and, therefore, the town with his own money, however, was a big deal. Not so much a foolish risk as a grand gesture.

An odd gesture from a man who didn't like it here.

Unless he was lying to her about his reasons? Or, maybe, keeping something from her?

Julia only stared at him for a moment before she asked, ''What else?''

Brock smiled casually. ''What else, what?''

Suddenly the office door burst open. Expecting to see Mary, Julia turned and saw Ian Roberts, instead. He stopped dead in his tracks. ''Julia.''

''Hi, Ian,'' she said, feeling awkward, because all three of them knew she was working for his father and living in the Roberts house to make up for the fact that Ian had cheated her out of a scholarship.

''It's nice to see you,'' he said stiffly, obviously uncomfortable, too.

''It's nice to see you, too,'' she countered, smiling, trying to lighten the mood. But the tension in the room was so palpable Julia felt pressure against her chest and it bothered her to the point that she couldn't take it. ''Oh, geez, Ian,'' she said, rising from her seat to walk over to face him. ''You and this damned scholarship thing are going to be the death of me.'' She reached out and hugged him. ''Will you ever forget this so I can get some peace?''

Smiling sheepishly, he pulled away from her. "It was the fact that I couldn't forget it that made it so I never got a minute's peace."

"Ian," Julia said quietly, realizing his genuine regret was reason enough that he deserved the truth. "This might be hard for you to understand, but that scholarship became the least of my worries the day I realized my mother was going to die. And I never gave it another thought. Not even a passing thought. Bigger problems always pushed it out of the way. Eventually time blotted it out completely."

Ian shook his head. "Maybe for you, but not for me. No matter how big my problems got, cheating you was always right there with them. But if everything turns out okay with Zack's grandparents because Brock here has taught you how to beat them at their own game, then I'll consider us even."

Self-conscious that Brock had confided their *entire* deal to Ian, but not really angry about it since Ian was a co-conspirator in this problem, Julia said, "Yeah, well, he's been a fair teacher." But, Julia really didn't want to discuss Zack's grandparents with Ian, and she certainly didn't want to discuss her etiquette progress, so she walked away, took her seat again, hoping that would close the subject.

Intentionally or not, Brock took the hint. "Julia came in to tell me that Dad's operation's been scheduled for next week."

"Next week?" Ian gasped.

"Next week. And I didn't even get as far as getting a power of attorney signed." He glanced at Julia. "Julia and I were both afraid of upsetting Dad," he said, his eyes narrowing as if daring Julia to contradict him. Because this was a family affair, Julia didn't say a word of argument, but Brock's stretching the truth hiked her suspicion that he hadn't told her everything about why he needed to use his own money to save the company.

Ian sagged into a chair. "So what are we going to do?"

"I'm going to liquidate a few of my assets."

"You've already put the farm on the market," Ian protested, indignant. "I won't let you..."

"You don't have any say in it."

Ian shook his head. "Brock, I came up here to tell you that George MacMasters announced his retirement today. That means we've got to promote Arlen Johnson into his spot."

Julia watched the red rise from Brock's neck to his face, but when he spoke, it was calmly. "We've 'got to'? There's nobody else?"

"Seniority demands he get the post next."

"I see."

He said the words with such ominous quiet that Julia found herself holding her breath. Zack picked that precise minute to show Brock his artwork. He rose from his kneeling position and announced "Done," waving the piece of paper in the air.

Though Julia expected Brock to ignore Zack in favor of more important matters, Brock smiled pleasantly at Zack, rose from his seat and walked over to the low table. He stooped to Zack's level and examined the scribble.

"Well, Picasso, I think you've outdone yourself. Why don't you make me another?"

Zack shook his head. "Uh-uh."

"Okay. Then come sit," Brock said, lifting Zack from the floor. He took his time arranging Zack on his arm, took his time walking to the desk.

Finally, after sitting on the leather chair behind the big desk and leaning back as far as the chair could go, Brock asked, "There's no one with a better education to promote before Johnson?"

"Historically, our director of operations doesn't have to be well-educated, just knowledgeable and experienced. Johnson's both. He's been preparing himself for this position for the past thirteen years."

"And now that he has his chance, he's probably laughing outrageously that it's me who gets to promote him. He'll undoubtedly die of hysterics when he discovers it's me who's footing the bill for the renovations." Brock paused, closed his eyes for the briefest instant, then said, "Give him the job. Announce it this afternoon. Announce it loud and clear."

"But Brock . . ."

"Just do it."

Though Julia had happily missed breakfast the morning before, wild horses couldn't have kept her away from dinner that night. The fact that Brock was liquidating his own property to rebuild Roberts Industries was almost forgotten in the face of this new tidbit about Arlen Johnson. Not because she wasn't concerned about Brock using his own wealth, but more because the Arlen Johnson problem was personal. She sensed more than knew that this issue was a peek either into why Brock left, or why he stayed away. And Julia decided that one way or another she was hearing this story. But every time she tried to bring up the topic of Arlen Johnson, or even Roberts Industries, Brock changed the subject.

By the time they were in the living room sipping brandy, Julia was so frustrated she could have spit nails. "All right," she said, angrily realizing she'd absently agreed to drink brandy in the living room again, in spite of the fact that she'd promised herself she wouldn't do it anymore because the last time they'd ended up kissing passionately. "You have fifteen seconds to tell me your beef with Arlen Johnson or I'm setting this untouched glass of brandy on the coffee table and calling it a night."

"Julia, I'm not going to tell you about the problem between Mr. Johnson and me."

Instead of leaving, as had been her threat, Julia only deflated. "But why?"

"Because you already know enough of my family's problems," Brock pointed out casually as he sat on the couch beside her. "I'm not telling you this one." He paused, considered, then added, "And since you learned about this while you were in my family's employ, I'm going to ask you—on your honor—not to go inquiring around town about it, either."

Eyes narrowed, she glared at him. "That is so unfair."

Studying his brandy, Brock smiled. "You of all people have no room to talk about fair."

She gaped at him. "How can you accuse me of being unfair?"

He smiled again. "For one, I virtually had to browbeat you into realizing you would easily, happily, readily, help my family, even though you continually refused our help."

"That was different. I don't take charity. This is a simple question, and not a matter of curiosity, either. Something happened between you and Arlen, and if you'd explain it to me, maybe I could help you solve it."

"You couldn't," Brock said with unqualified authority, then brought the original subject back. "And my keeping this from you isn't different. Because not only did you refuse our help, but you came to this house with your own secrets, and plenty of them."

"I don't think so," Julia disagreed.

"Oh, really, Miss Smarty Pants," Brock said, shifting on the sofa so that he was facing her. "If you have no secrets, why don't you just explain to me why Zack's grandparents are seeking custody of Zack instead of his father?"

For a full thirty seconds, Julia only stared at him. Thinking he'd bested her, Brock said, "See. We all have our little secrets."

Julia blinked. "Brock, Zack's father is dead."

Chapter Twelve

Brock felt like someone had just kicked him in the stomach. "I'm sorry, I didn't know."

"Of course you didn't know," Julia responded, unapologetically blunt. "We haven't ever really had a conversation about *me*. Not that I'm complaining," she hastily added. "It's just that if there's anything our time together has clearly pointed out to me, it's that you have a one-track mind. Take care of your father and get your family's company going again, so you can get the hell back home to Boston. No time to get personal, friendly, along the way. Just get the business over with."

Even as she spoke, a myriad of information twisted in Brock's brain. Quickly sifting through it, he realized that Julia had suffered at least three major tragedies in her life, yet she didn't complain. And she certainly wasn't bitter. Things that might cause another person to give up fighting, she seemed to take in stride. Including the fact that the person who was supposed to be helping her didn't pay one whit of attention to her—at least none above and beyond the call of duty.

Suddenly nervous, he rose and began to pace. "Is that really how I behave?"

Calm, looking at Brock as if she couldn't understand why the truth was so difficult, she said, "Brock, you ... well ... yes."

"I'm sorry."

"Please don't be sorry. I know that you're busy. I honestly wasn't complaining. I was only trying to explain that I understand. That's all."

Awed by the fact that she'd been so tolerant with him, and at the same time stunned that he'd been so insensitive with her, particularly since he'd thought he was moving them toward a romantic relationship, Brock lowered himself to the couch beside her. "Maybe you shouldn't be so understanding."

"What? I'm supposed to sit you down and demand that you listen to my life story? For what purpose? My goals are the same as yours. I want to see your dad well, and I want to see the company back on its feet. And, just like you, I want to see both done as quickly as possible without any distractions."

Listening to her talk, Brock suddenly saw why it was so easy for her to rebuff him. He knew she was attracted to him. He even knew she liked him, maybe even a lot. He read that in her eyes, the way she looked at him when she didn't realize he could see. But the problem was, she didn't sense any reciprocal feelings from him. When she pulled away from a kiss, or walked away from an opportunity, she wasn't declining anything except sexual advances. It was no wonder she constantly shot him down. He deserved it.

Hesitantly, he said, "The other half of our mission is to get you ready to meet Zack's grandparents, and I'm starting to realize I'm failing miserably."

"You're doing fine," Julia assured emphatically.

"No, I'm not doing fine. How can I help you...how can you say I'm helping you...if I don't even know something as basic as the fact that Zack's father is dead?"

Embarrassed, obviously feeling that he'd put her on the spot, Julia raised her hands helplessly. "Brock, what do you want me to say?"

"I want you to tell me about yourself. About your life."

She gave him a blank look. "There's not much to tell."

He couldn't believe that. She sat beside him, wearing Angel's white cashmere dress, the dress Angel refused to wear because it molded itself to every curve of her body, just as it did to Julia's now. Brock had to admit this kind of dress really wasn't Angel's style. But on Julia, it was magnificent. Not only did it accent a figure just dying to be caressed, but it made Julia's red hair look almost radiant. She didn't have to wear much makeup. She was almost always smiling. And when she wasn't smiling, she was listening. Making everybody in the world feel important. It was no wonder Moe loved her. Her smile alone probably brought in enough business to pay all his utilities.

How could a woman as beautiful as Julia, as empathetic as Julia, as fun-loving as Julia, have nothing to tell? And how could he have been so wrapped up in his own problems that he never thought to ask before this?

"Tell me about Zack's father."

After sighing slightly in resignation, she said, "Zack's father, David, was a geologist, who worked for a strip mining company just over the county line. He came into the diner for lunch every day and we started seeing each other. I had no idea he was wealthy. He rented a cabin in the mountains, and he lived a very simple life. In the months we spent together, we fished, we hiked, we swam in the lake behind his house."

"That sounds very nice," Brock said, even as a streak of jealousy spiraled through him. Not because he was jealous that she'd had a relationship, but being involved in her first intimate, ultraprivate relationship was an experience Brock himself couldn't give her. Someone else had beat him to it.

Uncomfortable, he rose from the couch and walked to the fireplace. He knew he wasn't going to be the first for her in many areas, but there was a part of him that wanted to show her things, give her things, that no one else had ever shown or given her. He supposed those feelings arose as a logical extension of his role as her teacher, but he squelched them because they really had no place in this situation. Theirs would not be a forever kind of relationship. What he wanted from Julia was whatever happened naturally. To this point, nothing had happened naturally between them because he'd been insensitive, so he was being sensitive now to get them back on the appropriate path. Nothing more. Except, of course, to be her friend, which Brock considered to be a normal part of any romantic relationship. No matter how short.

"When I discovered I was pregnant, David asked me to marry him, and I agreed. We wanted a simple, uncomplicated life, because we really were two peas in a pod and all that great stuff, but when David made the trip home to break it to his parents that he was not only getting married, but they were going to be grandparents, he was killed in a motorcycle accident. I found out his parents were wealthy when I tried... *tried* to attend the funeral, and couldn't." She paused, and drew a long breath. "I wasn't welcome. I guess I do have a big secret, after all. I've never told anybody that."

Brock turned from his position at the fireplace and stared at her. "They didn't want you there?"

"They may have thought I was a gold digger, somebody more or less taking advantage of their misery." She shrugged. "I don't know. I'm not quite sure what they thought, but I do know I only made matters worse when I naively tried to explain that I was pregnant with David's child."

Brock snorted a laugh. "I'll bet that went over real well."

"You have to understand, I didn't look pregnant yet. And they didn't know who I was—David had never spoken of me."

"He'd never spoken of you?" Brock asked incredulously.

She shrugged again. "David never went home. He wasn't the kind to write. And I'm certain he didn't hold long phone conversations with his mother to tell her about his girlfriends. It neither shocked, hurt, nor insulted me to discover he had never told them about me."

Brock conceded her point with a nod. "So it's taken you three years to prove to them that David was Zack's father?"

"No. What happened was when I went home and I thought about David, about who he was and how he lived, I realized he had more or less rejected his parents' life-style. I knew that David's parents' involvement in Zack's life would have been minimal if David were alive, because David would have lived here, in Roberts Run. He liked it here. And that's why I will raise Zack here. Because this is where David would have wanted Zack raised. So I never went back. Never tried to contact them again. I figured when the time was right for the Whittakers to meet Zack, I'd just sort of know it instinctively."

"But they came looking for you."

She nodded.

"Why? Why, after three years—almost four—would David's parents come looking for you now?"

"David had a room...probably a suite of rooms...in his parents' house. They only recently decided to dismantle it. When they did, they not only found evidence that I existed, but they found a diamond. Proof of commitment. They asked for blood tests. I complied because I believe Zack has a right to know that side of his family. But when it comes to moving away, or allowing them to take Zack away, that I can't tolerate. They're going to have themselves the fight of the century."

Brock smiled. This was what he liked about Julia. She didn't give up. Not ever. Not about anything. Life was literally trying to beat the hell out of her and she simply refused to let it. "That's the spirit."

"So, why aren't you fighting Arlen Johnson?"

She changed the subject so quickly and so well, Brock only stared at her until he got his bearings. "This really isn't show and tell time, Julia."

"I told you my big secret," she taunted, with a smile that quite clearly expressed that she thought she'd bested him.

He sighed. "There's nothing to tell."

"Tell me, anyway."

Trying to downplay the topic, Brock meandered to the bar. "Why?"

"To see if I can help."

"Help what?" he asked casually as he pulled out the brandy bottle.

"Help the two of you fix your little misunderstanding."

Realizing she wasn't going to stop, Brock laughed. "It wasn't a *little* misunderstanding. It wasn't any kind of *misunderstanding*, at all. And it is not something that can be fixed. Not by you. Not by anybody."

"How do you know?"

"Because there's nothing to fix," he said, splashing brandy into two snifters. "Theoretically there really isn't a problem anymore because we don't associate. My life is in Boston. Arlen Johnson's life is here."

"Your life is here, too."

He shook his head, handed her a glass of brandy and sat beside her on the sofa. "No. My father's life is here. Ian's life is here. But my life is not here."

"It could be."

"Julia, quite frankly, I never did fit in here. Neither did Angel. She's in California. I'm in Boston. And we're both very happy. Why would I want to give up everything I have and everything I love, to come home to a town I don't like and spend the rest of my life either fighting or trying to fit in?''

Tilting her head as she considered that, Julia asked, ''For your dad?''

''My dad doesn't need me as much as he thinks he does,'' Brock said, shaking his head at her persistence. ''After this operation, he'll be strong as an ox. He'll take the reins of the company again. Or Ian will. I'll have it built up so well by the time I leave, it will never be in danger of failing again.''

''Fairly sure of yourself, aren't you.''

He smiled devilishly. ''I'm that good.''

Julia couldn't help it, she laughed. ''You're awfully conceited, too.''

''But you like me, anyway,'' Brock said with unqualified authority, and Julia felt her heart jolt. She knew she didn't wear her emotions on her sleeve. She knew a person had to be able to read her expressions very well to know what she was thinking. She also knew that a smart woman would leave this very second while she still had some semblance of her heart intact.

He'd just told her he didn't ever want to live here, didn't want to leave behind the wonderful life he'd made for himself—particularly not to step into a difficult life in a small town. And she'd just told him she believed it would be David's wish for Zack to be raised in the town David had adopted for his home, the same way Brock had adopted Boston. She'd made it very clear that she was fighting the Whittakers not for her own wishes, but for David's.

Yet, here they sat, two millimeters away from kissing.

She pulled back.

''Brock,'' she said, characteristically open. ''I do like you a lot. Too much,'' she said, and rose from the sofa. ''I could fall for you in a heartbeat, and I think you're starting to feel something for me, too.''

He set his brandy on the table, leaned back on the sofa and stretched his arms across its back. He looked lean and sexy. He knew she was about to argue with him, so his eyes had taken on a predatory gleam. She sensed rather than knew that he didn't agree with her assessment of their relationship. She knew he would argue. She also knew he was giving her the opportunity to state her case first.

She almost wished he had an argument good enough to change her mind. Because she knew he didn't, she plunged ahead.

"In so many words you've just told me that you're going back to Boston."

He conceded that point with a nod. "In a few months."

"And I've quite plainly told you that I'd never leave here," she said honestly.

"So this means you're totally and completely opposed to any sort of relationship while I am here."

"I had my heart broken royally when Zack's father died." She shook her head helplessly. "I lost my best friend, my companion. I won't go through torment like that again."

"What makes you so sure I'm going to hurt you?"

"How can you possibly think you're not?"

He was beside her before she realized what was happening. He slid his hand along her nape, under her hair. Without a word, he gazed into her eyes with a look that was so deep and penetrating, it was primitive. "I don't agree with you. Not because I don't see the inevitability of parting, but because I think we have something to give each other. We could be good together," he said, his eyes smoldering. "Very good."

"For how long?" she countered. Her voice quivered from the strain of keeping herself physically and emotionally distant from him. Every fiber of her being longed to reach out to him, to take what he was offering, if only because she was a normal, healthy woman who was unbearably attracted to him. Not just his physical perfection, but his strength, his character, his odd sense of humor, his ability to handle Zack without a second thought. There were a million things to love about this man. And she was susceptible to all of them.

"Does it matter? Can't you just enjoy the moment?"

"No. Life's been a little too hard on me, Brock."

"Maybe it's because you've never learned to take your pleasure where you can."

"A few months' pleasure is hardly worth the years of heartache. Don't forget this is me you're talking to, Brock," she said, pointing at her chest. "I'm not a naive schoolgirl. I know what it really means to be lonely... to be alone."

"Did you ever stop to think that you are alone because you won't give any relationship a chance?"

"A chance? This isn't a game. You and I are a losing proposition. You're a fool if you don't realize that the logical conclusion to any kind of relationship between us is that one or both of us will be hurt." She stepped away from him. Nothing had ever been so difficult. Her skin still tingled from his touch. Her body still yearned for his. But emotionally, they were on two different planes. It was a gap she knew would never be bridged. "Good night, Brock."

Brock watched her walk out of the room, then sank down on the sofa. Her all-or-nothing attitude was nothing but a Roberts Run perspective. An outdated, outmoded frame of mind every bit as outdated and outmoded as most of the equipment at the factory. Brock could buy new equipment and make the company as competitive as the best corporation around. Changing the way Julia looked at the world wouldn't ever be that simple.

But he wasn't done with her yet. The only problem was, he had absolutely no idea what his next move should be. He only knew he never gave up on anything this easily. Especially not something he wanted so much.

Chapter Thirteen

On her way to breakfast the next morning, Julia met Frank in the hall. "What are you doing up?" she asked incredulously.

"I virtually slept away the past two weeks," he said, and motioned for her to precede him down the hall. "I'm feeling wonderful, fit as a fiddle, and I thought I'd join you and Brock for breakfast."

"That's great," Julia said sincerely. Not only was it good to see Frank so exuberant, but his presence might just take the edge off her meeting with Brock this morning.

"You're looking particularly striking today," Frank said as they began to descend the stairway.

"Thank you," Julia said. She'd taken to wearing Angel's clothes all the time now. Mostly because it was uncomfortable eating in the huge formal dining room in jeans and ragged sweatshirts, and partially because she was determined to learn how to live, behave and dress like someone the Whittakers would consider a good caretaker for their grandson. This morning she'd chosen white wool slacks and a rich cocoa brown sweater so soft it felt like silk against her naked back.

Unfortunately, she knew she looked a little better than she normally did and she'd fretted that Brock might take that the wrong way. She'd chosen the outfit the day before and didn't have enough time to sneak into Angel's room, get another set of clothes, change, and still be on time for breakfast.

When she and Frank walked into the dining room, Brock was staring out the huge bay window watching the quiet first-of-April rainstorm. He turned when he heard them, and Julia never knew if it was her outfit or Frank's appearance that caused Brock almost to do a double take. Ignoring his reaction, Julia confidently walked to her seat.

"Well, good morning to both of you," Brock said pleasantly, and Julia breathed a sigh of relief. As was his practice, he pulled out Julia's chair for her. Then, giving his father the seat at the head of the table, Brock walked to the other side and took the seat across from Julia, putting himself directly in her line of vision.

"To what do we owe the honor of your presence, Dad?"

"I feel great," Frank announced in his booming voice. "I feel so great that I didn't want to be cooped up in that room another minute."

"That's terrific," Brock said.

"And I also feel so great that I think it's time the three of us had a little talk."

Julia snuck a peek at Brock, trying to let him know with her eyes that she had no idea what was going on. Brock responded by giving her a similar look. Though the gesture had begun as perfectly innocent, somehow their gazes changed. She knew hers softened, but Brock's became charged with life and energy, and Julia felt trapped, hopelessly lost in Brock's beautiful brown eyes.

Frank slapped the table with his hand. "All right. First order of business," he said as Jeffrey entered the room. "Get Brock a place setting."

"Very good, sir," Jeffrey said happily. "And you'll be having your usual?"

"Yes, get me the damned oatmeal."

"Some people like oatmeal," Julia pointed out around a giggle.

"People without teeth like oatmeal. Anybody else who tells you that is lying," Frank said, then reached out and squeezed Julia's hand. "But don't get me off the subject. I know Brock has fifteen minutes before he'll be having a nervous breakdown from wanting to get to work so I need all this time to get everything out quickly."

This time, Julia didn't risk a look at Brock. Instead, she smiled at Frank and said, "Okay."

"Good. Now, Julia, I talked with Angel last night and she told me she would like for you to keep her clothes. *All* of her clothes."

"What?" Julia gasped. "I can't..."

"Julia, Angel is in a convent. She doesn't need these clothes. She told me last night she's decided to take her final vows."

"That's great, Dad!" Brock said, his excitement so evident Julia only stared at him.

"Yeah, wonderful. I have three kids. Two of you refuse to get married. The third joined a convent. I stand as much chance of having grandchildren as the Pope. I'm elated."

Julia couldn't help it, she laughed. Though Frank was grousing, Julia heard the note of pride in his voice. She patted his hand. "Don't give up on Ian, yet. After all, he's only my age, twenty-five, and I haven't given up on having more kids."

"Yeah, and by the time he gets married and decides to have kids I'll probably be dead and gone...."

"Dad, you've got to stop saying things like that," Brock interrupted. "You scared the hell out of Zachary the first day I was here by talking about dying. Now that I know his father is dead, I think I understand why."

Looking astounded, Julia glanced over at Brock, and he smiled at her. *Point one,* he thought, suddenly feeling victorious. Rome wasn't built in a day, and one conversation certainly wouldn't make him look sensitive, but taking something from an old conversation and linking it with something in a current conversation...now, that was a real work of art. And that went a long way not only to prove he'd paid attention to everything she'd said the night before, but that he understood.

"Humph," Frank grunted, then almost reached for a muffin, but caught himself. "I never thought of that." He turned to Julia. "I'll be more careful."

"I've never hidden from Zack that his father died, Frank. You can't protect your children from life. David's death is a part of Zack's life."

"Yeah, well, my death isn't really all that imminent, and I should have realized talking like that would have scared him. I won't do it again," he said, then turned to Brock. "But changing the subject doesn't free you from your responsibilities. Damn it, Brock, you're almost thirty-two. I never argued when you decided to leave. Never forced you home. The least you can do is find a woman and give me grandkids."

Brock smiled at Julia again. "I'm not quite ready for kids yet. I don't think there's anything wrong with wanting to spend special, private time with a woman before you make that kind of commitment."

"Only that the years are slipping by you, Brock," Frank grumbled, but Brock was more interested in watching the color rise in Julia's cheeks. As far as he was concerned, this didn't have to be complicated. She made it complicated. What he wanted was perfectly normal. And she wanted it, too. She just wanted it to come with a gilt-edged vow. A vow that would be incredibly premature given that they'd only met a few weeks ago.

"But we'll have to finish that discussion later," Frank said. "Or I won't get to the other more important things I have to talk about this morning. Julia, I think it's obvious that Angel doesn't need her clothes. Please take them and get some good use out of them."

"Thank you," Julia said.

"Okay, next subject. Brock, Ian tells me you promoted Arlen Johnson."

"Ian told me it was protocol and that I almost had no choice."

Frank nodded. "Actually, that's true. I want you to have a talk with him, though. He's been a supervisor for years, but he's been a little too tight with the employees. As director of operations, he's got to distance himself, start making decisions that benefit the company as well as the employees." He paused, considering, then said, "I know I don't have to explain this to you, but just so we're both clear on how I want this company run, I'm going to explain it, anyway. Somehow the scales have always got to be balanced. If we make every decision based only upon employee considerations, and we run the company in a lopsided way, those same employees may not have jobs a few years down the road. If we don't take care of reserves and put profits away for repairs and renovations, there won't be a Roberts Industries ten years down the road."

"Actually, Dad," Brock said carefully, glancing at his father. "You're getting precariously close to not having a Roberts Industries right now," he said, congratulating himself on the delicate use of understatement. "I'm working up a proposal for some renovations. I may even approach the bank for a loan so we can start upgrading while I'm here." He saw the confused look Julia gave him, and added, "But I'll only approach the bank as a failsafe mechanism. In case I don't find enough money in other tills."

For a moment, Frank seemed taken aback, but he recovered quickly. "Well, that's great, Brock, but I don't want to upgrade the factory if it means paying back loans. I don't think our income can sustain paying back a loan."

"I think with the right improvements we can upgrade the factory in such a way that we can increase our income. Then we not only would be able to pay back a loan, but we would increase our profits."

Frank turned to Julia. "That's why we sent him to Princeton."

"So I see."

Frank faced Brock again. "Then you're comfortable with renovating?"

"More or less," Brock said, edging around the truth—the tight deadlines, the fact that they may or may not be getting a fairly big government contract—because though his father seemed fine, he still had surgery scheduled for the next week. "Just give me something of a free hand for the next two months and I'll be happy."

"Good enough. And in exchange for permission from me to do anything you like with the company, I'd like a favor from you."

Brock responded without thinking. "Anything."

"Don't sell the Connor place."

"Dad..."

"Now, hear me out," Frank said, holding up his hands defensively. "I owe this little lady here a great deal for what she and Zack have done to restore my spirits in the last few weeks," he said, patting Julia's hand. "If we put a couple thousand dollars into renovations on that house, we could let Julia live there rent free...."

Julia gasped, interrupting him. "Frank, I can't let you..."

"You don't have much say in this. That farm's the perfect place to raise kids. And there's no way in hell the Whittakers could argue that you're not providing for Zack. We'll draw up an agreement that lets you live there as long as you need to and that will show the kind of stability no judge or court can argue.''

Awestruck, Brock sat back in his chair, wondering why the hell he hadn't thought of this first. It was perfect. Julia was looking for a commitment of sorts from him, and giving her a house was certainly a commitment. It wasn't marriage, but it was proof that they'd have a future. Now she didn't have any excuse under the sun for refusing to pursue this relationship.

"I agree with my dad," Brock said suddenly. He knew he'd have to sell a block of Compu-Soft to make up for the money he'd lose on the sale of the farm, but right now, at this moment, losing part of Compu-Soft didn't bother him.

"And I absolutely refuse to take your charity," Julia said, and rose from her seat.

"It's not charity," Frank argued. "In exchange for living on the farm, you'll be dropping by the house at least once a week. Mrs. Thomas and Jeffrey are getting too old to work twelve-hour days. I want to start giving them time off. So you'd be working for me in the evenings. Coming here while they were out—since I know you work daylight at Moe's." He paused and gave Julia a pleading look. "Julia, I'm an old man. I don't like to be alone. I love your son. I need someone to take care of me. Trust me, it's not charity."

This time when Julia entered Roberts Industries, she didn't wait for Nadine to greet her. She strode by the stunned blonde and up the steps. She also didn't pay any attention to Mary as she said, "Can I help you?" Instead, she marched past Brock's secretary, shoved open the door and entered Brock's office like a tornado touching down in the heartland.

"What in the hell do you think you're doing not selling that farm so I can live on it?"

Brock scrambled off his chair and closed the door as quickly as he could, while Julia continued to rant.

"You know I can't refuse your father the opportunity to spend time with Zack, especially after all his complaints about having no grandchildren. I was counting on you to turn into your normal self and remind your father that your life was your life and if you wanted to sell your farm, you would. Instead, you turned on me."

"I didn't turn on you."

"Didn't turn on me?" Julia gasped, staring at him. "How can you say that?"

"Very easily. I don't think that offering someone a home is turning on them."

"It is when the involved someone doesn't want the home."

"Why not?" Brock asked. Tired of watching her pace, he stopped her by standing in front of her, and kept her from turning away and walking in the other direction by putting his hands on her shoulders. Standing that close, looking into her mysterious eyes, feeling the tickle of the feathery ends of her hair as they grazed his knuckles, Brock found himself falling victim to temptation. He wasn't quite sure what it was about this woman that seemed to weaken his defenses so quickly and so easily, but whatever it was it was powerful. Looking into her green eyes, his mind went blank, instinct kicked in, and he bent his head and touched his lips to hers.

Partially expecting to get his face slapped, Brock was pleasantly surprised to feel her small hands creeping up his shoulders on their way to twine around his neck. He wasn't quite sure if he was rewarding her, or thanking her, for that gesture when he deepened the kiss. He only knew that he was awfully damned glad he'd closed and locked the door. He was feeling things he hadn't felt in a long time. Normal, natural male instincts that hadn't exactly deserted him in recent years, but simply weren't as intense as they were right now. He knew she felt this, too. He knew she liked him and wanted him as much as he liked and wanted her. He'd thought he was tired of her cat-and-mouse game, but it wasn't a cat-and-mouse game, anymore. Everything had taken on a new dimension since breakfast. He'd made a concession. Now it was her turn.

Pulling his mouth away from hers only far enough to speak and not so far that his mouth couldn't brush her lips as he formed the words, Brock said, "Don't you understand that I want you to take that house out in the country so we'll at least have a chance?"

She edged away from him. "A chance for what?"

"A chance to enjoy what we have. To be committed to each other."

"In other words, your giving me a house is something like a commitment to you?"

"Yes," Brock said, relieved that she'd finally caught on. "That's exactly it."

Without fully realizing what was happening, Brock began to notice the way her chest rose and fell. He saw her lips thin and her eyes narrow, as if she were angry. He decided she must not have understood what he had done for her and continued his explanation.

"Julia, your living in the house doesn't merely give me a reason, a real reason," he said, setting his hands on her shoulders again, "to come home. It'll bring me back here to visit more than twice a year. To spend more than just holiday time with my father. To actually have a vested interest in this area again. It also gives us a way to get to know each other away from prying eyes."

Her chin lifted. Cautiously, deliberately, she met his gaze. "Are you ashamed of me?"

"No. *No*," Brock said vehemently, though he suddenly felt like a man who'd stepped in quicksand and he wasn't even sure how or when. "I just don't want anybody...no, I don't *like* having anybody know my business."

"So, if I become your business, you don't want anybody to know. Yet you don't think I should feel you're ashamed to be involved with me."

"That isn't the way it is! I also don't want anybody to know how heavily I'm investing in the company, but you seem to understand that."

"I understand that you're keeping your investment quiet because you don't want anybody to realize Roberts Industries came about an inch away from going bankrupt. You don't want people worrying about their jobs."

She turned and stormed toward the door. "Giving me a house isn't the same, Brock. Not even close."

Julia walked out of Brock's office with her head high and proud, but outside the building, she slumped against the brick wall. Brock didn't have a clue about how he'd insulted her because part of his reasoning was right. He would visit more often if she took that house. And Frank would benefit.

But she would die. Before they even gave their relationship a chance, taking that house would give him the easy way out. He would have her, he would have Zachary, and he would have his father again. But he'd also have his life in Boston.

She'd be wholly committed to him, dedicated, waiting and watching for him to come home.

But he'd already be home...in Boston.

Taking that house would bind her to him as surely as any marriage vow, even as it gave him his freedom.

Chapter Fourteen

"Your father is in recovery now."

Julia took a long gulp of air and looked at Dr. Rose Morgan, who had finally finished Frank Roberts's surgery. Though uncomplicated and not dangerous, the procedure had been pushed back from its early morning schedule to a late afternoon time slot. Then, to make matters worse, it had lasted much longer than either Julia, Brock or Ian had expected. Though Ian and Julia seemed to be able to handle the delay with cautious optimism, Brock virtually crawled out of his skin.

"Can we see him?"

"You can see him," the doctor said, "but he probably doesn't want to see you as much as he wants to sleep right now. If I were you, I'd sneak in, tell him good night, and then go home and get a good night's sleep yourselves. I can guarantee you he's going to look better and feel better in the morning."

"I think she's right, Brock," Julia said carefully, touching Brock's sleeve to get his attention.

"Yeah, so do I, Brock," Ian agreed. "Let's go in, say good night, and then come back in the morning."

At first Brock looked reluctant to agree. But fourteen hours in a hospital waiting room had worn him down to the point that rather than actually agree, he merely seemed too tired to argue.

Doing as the doctor instructed, the trio spent only a few minutes with Frank then left the hospital. Without a word, they walked to Brock's Mercedes. Ian immediately took the back seat, since they'd be letting him off first, which forced Julia into the front seat with Brock.

Ian made small talk for the thirty minutes it took to get from the hospital to his house. When he got out of the car, it became eerily quiet.

Sitting in the silent vehicle, with darkness fully descended around them, Julia felt her first prickle of discomfort. She and Brock hadn't really spoken since their argument in his office. Not because they hadn't seen each other. They had. Every morning they ate breakfast together. Every evening they ate dinner. But until last night, Frank had joined them, and he managed to make the meals comfortable and happy—and kept them from discussing the topic too delicate for Frank only days away from surgery.

Since Frank was in the hospital last night, Julia didn't have dinner with Brock, but had taken Zack to Moe's for a burger and then to the hospital for a visit with Frank to prove to Zack there was nothing to worry about. Then Brock and Julia had missed eating breakfast together this morning because Brock needed to go into the office to make sure everything would be okay without him for a day. Now, for the first time since a passionate kiss and an insult that negated it, they weren't merely alone. They were alone on a dark road, in a very quiet car.

"Would you like some music?" Julia asked suddenly, not only to get rid of the silence, but also as a signal of sorts that she didn't hold any grudges and planned to be agreeable and pleasant for the few days Frank was in the hospital.

"No," Brock said quietly. "I just want some peace and quiet."

Understanding that, and also understanding that was Brock's way of telling her she didn't have anything to worry about from him, Julia settled back in her seat. She knew he didn't understand how much he'd insulted her, and it would be demeaning to have to explain that giving her a house, but not making a home with her, was nothing but an empty promise. So she sat quietly, accepting their mutual concessions as a truce of sorts.

But in spite of the shaky peace between them, the ten-minute drive from Ian's house to the Roberts residence passed slowly. Once the Mercedes was parked in the multi-car garage, Julia jumped out and started walking toward the door to the house.

"Good night, Brock," she called. "I'll see you in the morning."

"What?" Brock said, sounding disoriented. "Wait. I was going to make us something for supper."

Julia glanced at her watch. "But it's almost nine o'clock."

"And you haven't eaten yet, so you must be hungry."

She was hungry, but she also had planned on slipping away from Brock and sneaking down for a midnight snack once he'd settled in for the night. Watching him slowly walking from the car, Julia felt a tug at her heartstrings. His face, blackened by the whiskery shading of a five o'clock shadow, was solemn and drawn. Because of his unbuttoned black wool topcoat, Julia could see his loosened tie and his partially unbuttoned shirt.

She'd never seen him look like this, but somehow, in some way, his sloppiness was endearing. He looked tired, and in need of comfort, if not simple companionship. No matter how dangerous it was to her own heart, she knew she couldn't deny him. Not tonight. "Yeah, I guess you're right," she said. "I could use a sandwich."

He paused in front of her, slid his key in the lock, then glanced over his shoulder at her. "I was going to make stir-fry."

Surprised, but hiding it well, Julia said, "That would be great."

"Good," he said, pushing open the door and granting her entrance. "Give me two minutes to get out of this suit."

Julia decided to change clothes, too. Though Angel's navy blue blazer and trousers were adequately comfortable, they weren't the kind of clothes Julia would cook in. But more than that, Julia didn't feel like trying to be somebody she wasn't tonight. Frank's operation might have been simple and safe, but it was still an ordeal. He was a friend and Julia had worried about him. Tonight, right now, she simply wanted to be comfortable. Sneaking up the back-stairs, she slipped into her room, kissed sleeping Zachary's cheek, then put on a pair of loose-fitting jeans, a warm sweatshirt and old, comfortable slipper socks.

When she returned to the kitchen, Brock was already chopping vegetables. Pushing through the kitchen door, Julia stopped dead in her tracks. Not only because he looked perfectly normal chopping green peppers behind the pristine white ceramic tile butcher block, but because he, too, had on jeans and a sweater. They weren't as grungy as the paint-splattered set he'd worn on the visit to the Connor farm. They were normal jeans and a normal sweater. The kind a normal person would wear. And he looked great. Better than great. He looked approachable. Normal. He looked like someone she could spend the rest of her life with.

Dangerous thought, she decided as she walked into the kitchen. "What can I do to help?"

"Pull up a chair and start talking about something that will take my mind off my father."

"Brock, your father is going to be okay."

"I know that. That's why I want to take my mind away from all the odd possibilities that keep creeping into my brain."

Strips of lean beef were sizzling in a frying pan on the white stove. Brock turned and tossed in the peppers, then lowered the temperature for the burner as if he'd been doing this all his life.

"Where'd you learn to cook like this?"

Glancing up at her, he smiled. Some of the tiredness had gone from his face. A little of the light had returned to his eyes. "I do live alone, you know."

"You seem like the type to eat out every night."

"Eating out every night gets old fast."

"Hmmm, I'd like the opportunity to experiment with that one."

"You may get it when you go to Connecticut."

"I don't want to talk about that."

"Okay, I don't want to talk about my dad. You don't want to talk about Zack's grandparents. That leaves us with ... ?"

"Well, I don't really know a lot about your life in Boston."

"Fair enough," Brock agreed, chopping onions. "I own the controlling interest in Compu-Soft, the company I run, even though I sold off a large block of the stock last week to make up for the money I lost from not selling the Connor place."

Julia let that comment slide because she knew Brock had not meant for it to be inflammatory. He didn't want to argue any more than she wanted to argue. They were just two people trying to get through the night.

"I keep an apartment in the same building that houses the Compu-Soft offices, but I also have a house in the country. That's where I live when the weather permits me to live there.

"It's nice, it's beautiful. Not a house like this one," he said, glancing around at the completely white kitchen, so bright its artificial light almost hurt his eyes. "It's not huge and ostentatious and grand. Though I have five bedrooms, everything is cleanly drawn and simple. I don't have extravagant taste like my mother did." Considering that, he looked up at Julia and smiled. "Zack would be very happy in my house."

Knowing she couldn't touch that comment, either, Julia ignored it. "Your mother was responsible for all of this, then?" she said, referring to the huge, well-decorated house in which Frank Roberts lived.

"Up until the day she died, she was redecorating, considering every possibility for all the rooms. She loved this house. She loved having something this huge to fill."

Julia heard the note of sadness in Brock's voice, and for the first time many things about Brock's attitude today began to take on meaning. Julia knew all about Penny Roberts's passing. She knew Brock's mother had died a slow, painful death. She also knew that Penny had gone into the hospital for routine surgery when they discovered her cancer.

"How old were you when your mother died?" she asked suddenly.

Brock shrugged. "I was already working for Compu-Soft, though I hadn't bought the company yet."

"Have you ever noticed that you relate everything back to your company?"

"It's the most important thing in my life."

"Then why have a house with five bedrooms?"

He shrugged again. "I live in the country, most of my friends can't afford to. I'm only a stone's throw away from riding stables and a lake. We have a lot of summer weekends, picnics, that kind of thing."

"Do you like it?"

"I did. I mean, I'm looking forward to summer again. But this year with Dad sick, nothing feels the same. Nothing feels right."

"That's understandable."

"Really?" he asked, turning away from her to finish his cooking.

"Sure," Julia said, and squirmed on her tall stool. "Brock, I'm not going to play stupid with you. I remember when your mother died. It was really sad. I think you're worried that something similar may happen to your father."

"I suppose you're right in a way," he agreed, but still busied himself with his sizzling pan and didn't face her. "It seemed like my mother was perfectly fine one day, and the next she was waiting to die. It was unbelievably traumatic. Being away didn't help much."

"Did you come home often?"

"Every weekend. In the beginning . . ."

"Why'd you stop?"

He shrugged. "I don't know."

"Of course you know," Julia said, pushing him. From her own mother's death, Julia knew that this was something he needed to talk about. "Brock, lots of people have trouble dealing with watching someone they love die. . . ."

"That's not it," Brock said, and pivoted to face her with such force, Julia didn't even see him move. "God, how shallow do you think I am?"

"Then what happened?" she asked, every bit as adamant as he was. "You don't stop visiting a dying parent for no reason."

Though he had been dishing out rice, he turned and looked her right in the eye, giving his statement more strength and meaning. "I couldn't stand to be here."

"Here? In this house?"

"Here in this town," he said, still looking her in the eye.

"But why?" she asked, totally confused. "Brock, the people who live in Roberts Run are good, simple people. I can't think of a thing anybody could do that would be so bad that you'd..."

"Oh, really, well try this on for size from your *good, simple* people," Brock said, angrily interrupting her, though he turned his attention back to serving their dinners. "I was at the pharmacy, picking up my mother's prescription...."

He paused as if he suddenly realized the momentum of their argument had carried him into telling a story he didn't want to tell. But Julia wasn't about to let him stop now. "And?"

He didn't answer for a few seconds, and when he did his voice was lighter, not angry anymore. Almost as if he'd pulled all the emotion from it. "And it wasn't ready so I decided to go over to Cattleman's Tavern for a beer," Brock said, then carried their two plates to the round table in the breakfast nook. "I hope you don't mind eating here tonight."

"Actually, this would be great. Wonderful."

Brock set the plates on placemats left on the table by Mrs. Thomas. Julia grabbed silverware from the drawer and paper napkins from a pantry and then joined Brock.

They sat down, divided the silverware, and Brock took a bite of his food. "Umm. Even after weeks of Mrs. Thomas's cooking, I haven't lost my touch."

Julia smiled craftily. "And you also haven't wormed your way out of finishing your story."

He gave her a blank look.

"You went to Cattleman's Tavern for a beer," Julia reminded him, though in her mind's eye she had trouble picturing Brock drinking beer, never mind trying to picture clean and neat Brock in a bar that prided itself on not having rest rooms. "And something happened."

He drew a long breath. "You know, I thought I could tell you this story, but it's not coming out as easily as I thought it would."

"You've never told anybody this?"

"Not a soul."

Biting her lip, Julia glanced at him again. "The sad routine's not going to get you out of this, either, Brock."

"Damn it, Julia, I just plain don't want to tell this story. I don't even know why I started it. I wish I hadn't. Back off, okay?"

"Did somebody say something to you?" An idea struck Julia and she amended her question. "Did Arlen Johnson say something to you?"

"No. Truthfully, I don't think anybody even realized I was in the bar until I grabbed Arlen by the throat and threatened to punch his face in."

Julia groaned. "Come on, Brock, you can't tell me this much of a story and then tell me to mind my own business."

He sighed heavily. "All right, but Julia, this is really an awkward, difficult memory," he said, and from the expression on his face, Julia knew he'd only given in because he didn't have the energy tonight to argue with her. By the way his voice lightened again, Julia sensed that he was also about to downplay the situation into being much less traumatic than it actually had been. "Once I tell you, you have to promise me that you'll drop it."

Though she wasn't sure it was a promise she could keep, Julia said, "Word of honor."

"Okay," Brock said, then drew another long breath. "I walked into the bar, and Johnson and his crowd were at a round table in the corner, playing cards. Though it was only about one in the afternoon, they were drunk and they were kind of shoving at each other." He paused and ran his hand across his mouth, but Julia didn't say anything. Instead, she kept her gaze locked on him, letting him know she wasn't saying anything or eating a bite until he finished this story.

"Anyway, they were looking for some kind of game to play. I guess they'd been there all morning and were bored. One comment led to another, and the next thing I heard was that they'd decided to have a pool for the day my mother would die."

Julia's eyes widened in horror. "Oh, Brock, that's awful."

"Everybody was going to chip in a hundred dollars, and, of the five men sitting at the table, the one who came closest to the day of my mother's death would get the five hundred. So I stormed over, yanked Johnson out of his chair and threatened to punch his face in. The next thing I knew I was sitting on the sidewalk in front of the bar. *I'd* been thrown out for starting a fight."

"Brock, I'm so sorry. But I'm sure they didn't mean..."

"Of course they didn't mean anything by it. To them, my mother's death was nothing but an object for a game, because to most of them, my family was...*is*...nothing. Not real. Sort of not people. You and I know we're just like everybody else, but in this town we're considered different from the rest of the community because they don't *want* us to be like them.

"They want to be able to legitimately dislike us if things don't go as they think they should at the factory. They want to be able to go into the bar and blow off steam. They want to be able to make fun of us, because to them it's nothing more than a game. They don't want to get to know us, they certainly don't want us to integrate into their community, and to be frank and blunt, hiding out in a big house, with very little human contact, isn't very much of a life. It's why I can't stay, Julia," he said, locking his gaze with hers. "And it's why I don't want anyone knowing anything about me or my family that they don't have to know."

Chapter Fifteen

A week later, Brock was sitting at the desk in his father's office, trying to focus on the brochure for machinery he planned to buy, but all he could think about was Julia. He'd been cool to her for the first two days after she forced him to bare his soul, but she'd brought him around slowly, and last night they'd laughed like two damned fools over dinner. Then, today, the oddest thought occurred to Brock. Even letting her know the worst secret of his past hadn't made him feel uncomfortable around her. If anything, now that the cold war was over, it might have made him *more* comfortable around her.

He sat back in his chair and closed his eyes. He still wanted her. There were nights he was *crazy* with wanting her. And now that she seemed to have forgotten that his family had offered her a house, which she regarded as charity, maybe tonight should be the night—not to try to seduce her, but to get their relationship back on the right track. At the very least, to remind her that he hadn't changed his mind about wanting her. And, maybe, just maybe, to get her to think about wanting him, too.

His thoughts were interrupted by the ringing of his private line, and he answered immediately, "Brock Roberts."

"Brock, this is Harvy. How are you? Better yet, how's everything going down there?"

"Fine, Harvy," Brock said, and sat back on his chair. "What's up?" he asked carefully, knowing Harvy wouldn't have called without good reason.

"Well, I guess I have good news and bad news."

"What's the good news?"

"The good news and the bad news are the same. Roberts Industries is the only bidder on the contract I told you about."

Brock didn't bother asking Harvy how he knew. Harvy had connections all over the place, and if he said Roberts Industries was the only bidder, then Roberts Industries was the only bidder. "That means we'll probably be getting that contract."

"Unless your numbers are way off base, you're the one, Brock."

"Lord," Brock said, squeezing his eyes shut. "This means I have to have my renovations done by the first week of September."

"No, this means your renovations have to be done *and* your new equipment tested by the first of September." Harvy paused. "Do you, at least, have your factory layout plan?"

"Yes. The project's out for bid already."

"Any possibility of calling in the bids before the deadline?"

"No, but I can sure as hell make my decision more quickly." Brock stopped, considered, then said, "Actually, I can have a contractor in here in about two weeks."

"That sounds about right. How's your dad?"

"That's a whole different story."

"How so?"

"Well, the doctor tells me everything went well, but Dad's lethargic. Listless. It's like he doesn't want to come home, though he's scheduled to come home tomorrow."

"Do you know why?"

Brock blew his breath out on a quiet sigh. He knew why. Though Julia hadn't come right out and said it, the whole family knew Julia wasn't going to take the Connor house. To her it wasn't just charity, it seemed to be some kind of an insult. As far as Brock was concerned, the subject was better left dropped. And though Frank seemed to sense that, too, he was still upset about it—in spite of Julia's constant chatter about being a regular visitor once she got back from Connecticut.

"Well, give him a hell of a coming home party," Harvy said when Brock didn't answer. "And then give him a reason to get better once he's home, because you're gonna need him."

When Brock returned from work that day, Julia met him at the door. Dressed in a black pleated skirt, white turtleneck sweater and a long black jacket, with her hair pulled into a tight chignon, she looked more like a schoolteacher or secretary than a woman dressed for dinner.

"What's up?" Brock asked. She looked so cute he just barely resisted the urge to kiss her hello. But resist he did, because all his plans for tonight had gone down the toilet with one simple phone call. If what Harvy said was true and Roberts Industries got that contract, Brock's father had to be able to take over the factory this September. Worse, sometime within the next three—*three*—weeks, Frank had to be strong enough to hear the news that his workload would *triple* in a few months. For both of those to happen, Brock needed to talk Julia into taking the Connor place. If he didn't, Brock knew he might as well kiss Boston goodbye because Ian would never be able to handle this project alone.

"I have to ask a favor," she said solemnly.

"Sure. Anything," Brock said, and meant it. The best way to get somebody to do you a favor was to do one for them first. And before the night was over, Brock planned on convincing Julia that the Connor house should be her new home.

"I want Zack to eat dinner with us tonight."

Brock carefully held his smile in place to keep from grimacing. "What?"

"I think Zack needs to spend some time in the formal dining room with us . . . just in case."

"Okay," Brock agreed, cautiously, still managing to keep the distress out of his voice.

"That's why I didn't dress up too much," she explained as she helped Brock out of his topcoat and took it to the hall closet. "I don't want to go overboard and scare him." She paused, studied Brock's appearance, then said, "You could stay the way you are, if you don't mind not changing."

"I don't mind," Brock said, then swallowed hard. What Julia managed to do to him with a mere look was sinful. He knew she was only surveying his appearance for the purposes of considering whether he was adequately attired to help coach Zachary, but anytime she looked at him, appraised him, Brock's flesh warmed. The problem was no matter how much he needed her for business purposes, he still *wanted* her. Worse, he wanted her to want *him*. He wanted her to see him as more than just a friend or a help mate.

So, every time she looked at him, *any time* she looked at him, there was a chance that she'd see something that would change her mind about a romantic relationship, and Brock's imagination kicked into overdrive.

But he stopped it. He took those wicked thoughts and he ground them into the floor until they were as flat as pancakes, because he couldn't afford for her to walk out on him and, therefore, his father. Not when they were this close.

"Thanks," she said, then stood on her tiptoes and kissed his cheek before jogging up the spiral staircase.

Just on the brink of being aroused from a simple cheek kiss, Brock watched her go. He was either going to have to talk himself out of liking her, talk her into a conditional relationship, or forget about saving Roberts Industries and return to Boston before she drove him crazy. Because he was never going to stop wanting her. That much was patently clear.

He entered the formal dining room and immediately noticed that the table was set with three places. He strode to the buffet and poured himself a small glass of wine. Before he'd fully filled his glass, he heard Julia and Zack entering.

When he glanced at the door, the sight that greeted him was so profound, he had to set his wine on the buffet again. Prim and proper, straight and tall, Julia held Zack's round little hand. But tonight the hand wasn't grubby. It wasn't even semisoiled. Dressed in a miniature black suit, with a red tie, Zachary looked like someone ready to start his first day at Compu-Soft.

"Zachary," Brock said, amazement dripping through his voice.

"Good evening, Mr. Roberts," Zachary said, then looked down at his shiny black loafers.

Brock walked to the doorway. "Good evening to you, too, Mr. MacKenzie," Brock said, and extended his hand to shake Zack's. Zack returned Brock's handshake, grinning as if he realized he had passed at least one test.

"It's a pleasure to have your company for dining this evening," Brock said, and, confused, Zack quickly glanced up at his mother.

She bent and whispered, "Just say thank you," and Zack immediately complied.

"Thank you," he said, then looked down at his shoes again.

"Somebody's done some excellent coaching," Brock commented as the three made their way to the table.

"We've spent a little bit of time every day practicing politeness," Julia explained, as Zack carefully guided himself to his seat at the table. "But we thought we needed an actual dress rehearsal."

"And it's my pleasure," Brock said, truly astounded that the demure child in the black suit was actually Zachary. "Here, let me help you," he added as Julia bent to lift Zack into a booster chair.

"Thank you," Julia said.

"Thank you," Zachary immediately parroted.

Hoisting Zack into his seat, Brock chuckled. "This kid is going to pass with flying colors."

"Hmmm," Julia murmured noncommittally. "We'll see how he does with the peas," she said as she turned to take her own seat.

"Peas?" Brock said skeptically, then rounded the table to his own chair.

"I've taken the liberty of setting the menu," Julia announced.

Mrs. Thomas entered, wearing her full dress uniform with the starched white collar and headpiece. She carried a tray with two salads and a dish of applesauce. Serving Julia first, she set a salad in front of her.

"You and I will have salads, Zack will have applesauce."

"That's good," Brock agreed, eying Zachary's white shirt and the brownish applesauce. He saw Mrs. Thomas unsuccessfully try to stifle a devilish grin. But when she set the applesauce in front of Zack and he gazed up at her and said, "Thank you, Mrs. Thomas," Brock watched Eleanore's eyes fill with tears.

Julia smiled, then faced Brock again. "If we're ever in a position where we must eat formally with the Whittakers, I plan to leave instructions with the staff to precut Zack's meat and to serve him softer, smaller cuts of vegetables.''

"That's very good," Brock agreed, truly impressed. He couldn't picture the Julia he'd met four weeks ago thinking this far ahead, let alone acting on her own strategy. Her preplanning was clear proof of how much she'd changed and how ready she'd become for this challenge. Reaching out, he patted her hand. "You both are doing beautifully."

Rather than duck her head at the compliment as Zack had done, Julia raised her head proudly. "Thank you," she said graciously, then she addressed Mrs. Thomas. "We'll ring when we're ready for the next course."

Brock felt as if the breath had been kicked out of him. Not only had Julia learned to behave with poise and confidence, but she had actually *become* poised and confident. Though he'd been the person to teach her most of what she now knew, Brock didn't feel there was any reason to take credit. This, he believed, was her natural state. She just needed the time to realize it for herself.

Still watching Julia in awe, the obvious struck Brock. She kept telling him he had to move back to Roberts Run for them to have a relationship. But she'd changed so much and so rapidly, that Julia herself might not find Roberts Run to be her home of choice fairly soon. Particularly not after she visited Connecticut. She could, realistically, some day want to move to Boston with him.

Without any strain to his imagination, Brock could see her in his house, hostessing his parties, sleeping on his black satin sheets. His breath lodged in his throat. He never realized how badly he wanted this—wanted her—but he also knew he had to tread lightly. Not only did he want a little time before he made that kind of commitment, but he also needed her in the Connor place. At least until his father was fully recovered.

True to Julia's plan, when dinner was served, Brock could see that Mrs. Thomas had cut Zachary's pork chop into small, child-sized bites. Zack's mashed potatoes had only enough gravy to enhance their flavor and not so much as to ruin his tie. His peas were in an easily accessible mound. His utensils were smaller, a proportion and shape that fit Zack's hand.

"So, Zachary," Brock said, turning the dinner conversation to Zack to allow him to share in the meal properly. "Did you do anything exciting today?"

"I rode a pig," Zack replied, then giggled.

"A pig?"

"Jeffrey played with him this afternoon," Julia explained, answering the skepticism on Brock's face. "Because Jeffrey was raised on a farm, he sometimes plays barnyard games with Zack. He's teaching him the sounds animals make and some of their characteristics and habits. Question Zack further and you're liable to discover that he also rolled around in imaginary mud."

"Really," Brock said, and Julia watched his lips arch into a huge smile.

Julia set her fork on her dish. "Brock, did you do anything normal as a child?"

"Not really, I guess," Brock said, shaking his head. It was strange, he realized, to talk to a woman who attracted him enough that he'd actually consider a permanent relationship. The first thing that hit him was that he had to be completely honest. So he was. "I spent so much time reading that I didn't have time for much else." He paused, considered, then added, "I suppose that's why I like to be outside so much now."

Zack's head jolted upward. "Outside?"

Before Julia could answer, Brock turned to Zack. "You know what, Zack," Brock said. "You've been doing so well here tonight, that I think you should be rewarded. And I'm going to give you a choice. I can take you outside tomorrow, or we can do something together tonight."

"It's better to reward him immediately for good behavior," Julia said with motherly authority.

"What can we do tonight?" Brock asked seriously.

"Well, we can take him in the family room and play a game with him—which will only teach him to play in his good clothes, and we don't want to do that, either," Julia said, giving Brock a telling look. "Or if you really want to reward him, he likes to go to Moe's for pie."

"Then Moe's it is," Brock agreed happily. "My treat," he added, turning to Zack.

Zack grinned. "Thank you, Mr. Roberts," he said, then laughed noisily, obviously thrilled by his success.

"He certainly catches on quickly."

"The reward system never fails," Julia said, then smiled at her son. Like it or not, they were on their way. As ready as they'd ever be. And so far, so good.

An hour later, Brock was pulling his Mercedes into one of the parking places in front of the diner, under a street lamp. Julia didn't question his caution or conservative attitude. In fact, she was almost a little puzzled by Brock's willingness to boldly enter Roberts Run. He wasn't nervous about being in town, as he had been when he talked of going to meet his lawyer only three weeks before. He hadn't even balked at the suggestion to go to Moe's. In the last few hours, Julia almost felt as if she were dealing with a different man. If parking under a streetlight to protect his car was his only concession, Julia was glad to make it.

Brock exited the Mercedes first and, after opening Julia's door for her, quickly opened the back door to lift Zack out of his car seat. Not wanting to destroy the mood or the moment, she didn't protest when he carried Zack to the diner door. Giggling, Zack pushed open the door for them, and, as it granted them entry, the little bell tinkled.

"Who's out there?" Moe yelped from his place in the kitchen.

"Put on your glasses and you'll be able to see us!" Julia called back.

Whatever utensil he was using hit the floor with a thud, and Moe scrambled out of the kitchen wiping his hands on his oversized white apron. "Julia," he cried, then he spotted Brock and Zachary and he stopped short. "Zack," he said with heartfelt emotion, clearly stunned by Zack's sparkling clean suit and prestigious-looking tie. "Brock," he added, sounding as astounded by Brock's presence as he was by Zack's neat appearance.

"Hello, Moe," Brock greeted cheerfully as he slid Zack onto one of the counter stools. He pulled Zack's little overcoat off his shoulders, then removed his own black wool overcoat and walked both to the rack close to the kitchen. When he returned, he took Julia's coat for her and placed it with his and Zachary's.

"What the hell is going on here?" Moe asked, obviously amazed. His well-lined face had puckered so much he looked like a man who'd eaten a very sour pickle. Half the pucker was from a need of his glasses, the other half was sheer surprise. "Brock," he said, scratching his bald head. "You haven't been in this diner in . . ."

"I haven't been here since right before my mother died," Brock supplied casually, then took the stool beside Zack. "We're having pie."

Moe looked at Julia and she only smiled, somewhat astounded herself. She'd like to think that her discussions with Brock had borne fruit and that he was starting to become more comfortable with his home, but she knew the truth. Zack was like a guru. Just as David had been able to make anyone, anywhere, comfortable, Zack had also been blessed with that gift. At least that's how she decided to credit Brock's change of heart. Because the alternative was to think that as he got reacquainted with Roberts Run, he was getting so relaxed he actually might be starting to like it. And Julia was smart enough to know that was nothing but wishful thinking.

She took the stool on the other side of Zachary. "I'll have blueberry... and coffee," she added, closing her eyes in anticipated ecstasy.

"Chocolate," Zack said, grinning.

"I like cherry. If I remember correctly, Moe, you make the best cherry pie in the county."

"You're damned right I do," Moe said, beaming with pride not merely over his pie, but also, Julia knew, over the fact that Brock had decided to visit him, if only because Brock was Frank's son and Frank was Moe's best friend.

After setting their pie in front of them, Moe reached for the coffeepot and said, "I was planning to visit your dad tomorrow afternoon, but when I called him, he told me he's coming out of the hospital in the morning."

"Yes, that's what the doctor told me this afternoon."

"Your dad never mentioned it," Moe said, "but I heard some rumors that it was really a rough operation. Lasted much longer than it should have."

Julia watched Brock absorb the fact that his father had been the object of gossip. He took the information in, swallowed his anger with a bite of pie, then smiled at Moe. "It was more difficult than we'd anticipated, but Dad is fine now."

Sobering, Moe leaned against the counter. "I'm so glad he pulled through all this."

"Me, too," Brock agreed. "The heart attack this winter was such a scare."

"Yeah, but your dad's too tough to die," Moe insisted good-naturedly. "He's a feisty old coot like me, and we've already decided to live forever."

"I wish you would," Brock said seriously. "And by the way, the pie is delicious," he added to change the subject.

Julia noted that Brock protected his privacy even as he protected Moe's feelings, and he did it without any emotion whatsoever. He didn't get angry. He didn't seem to feel put upon, or that his life had somehow been invaded. He simply did it. Seeing that, Julia felt odd, newly blossoming feelings for Brock the likes of which were even more foreign than wearing a suit to eat pie at Moe's. Those feelings inspired her to think things she hadn't dared think since she'd met Brock Roberts all those weeks ago. She was thinking things like how he could handle himself here in Roberts Run with a little patience and a little practice. She was thinking things like how much he actually liked it here in Roberts Run, but almost didn't seem to know it himself. And she was thinking things—dangerous things—like how he was bound to realize eventually that he really did belong here.

After eating his pie, and then putting two quarters in the jukebox and showing Brock how well he danced, Zack ran out of steam right before everyone's eyes. With a shared look, Julia and Brock scooped him up to take him home.

In the car, on the drive to the Roberts house, Julia got more of those odd feelings. Darkness and silence covered them in a blanket of security and contentment. Julia realized with a start that though David and Brock were completely different, the common trait they shared was the way their presence gave Julia a sense of rightness.

Odd. Several weeks ago, even several days ago, Julia never would have associated a sense of rightness to how she felt about Brock, but here it was. And smack dab up against that sense of rightness was the realization that she'd blocked any attempts Brock had made or suggested for them to fall naturally into the beginnings of a normal relationship.

Brock pulled his car into the garage and gently lifted Zack from his car seat. Julia walked ahead of them, opening doors and clearing pathways for Brock as he carried Zack to bed. After Julia pulled back his covers, Brock settled Zack against his pillow, and Julia immediately slid the loafers off.

From the corner of her eye, she watched Brock give Zack one last loving look, then he cleared his throat. "I guess I'll see you in the morning."

Julia paused, but only for a second. Placing Zack's shoes on the floor beside his bed, she said, "If you don't mind waiting while I slip Zack into pajamas, I wouldn't mind having a glass of brandy tonight."

Chapter Sixteen

Once Zack was comfortably settled, Julia slipped off the black jacket of her suit. She removed the pins from her hair, but rather than let it hang loose and wild, she pulled it up in a slack ponytail with a mane comb.

Eyeing herself critically in the vanity mirror, she decided that even without the jacket and with the more casual hairstyle, she still looked stiff and formal. Thinking this, she remembered a very comfortable-looking one-piece cotton outfit of Angel's. Without another second for deliberation of consequences or ramifications, she ran to Angel's room and found the slim yellow lounging pajamas. After removing her sweater and pleated skirt, she slid into the floral concoction and, again, eyed herself critically.

The one-piece outfit was made of lightweight but opaque yellow cotton. Mixed and mingled throughout the fabric were tiny red rosebuds. The outfit was sleeveless with a scoop neck, but it wasn't revealing. She truly didn't look like a woman who was out to seduce a man, only a woman who'd gotten comfortable.

And sticking with that rationalization, Julia marched downstairs.

She found Brock in the formal living room. Obviously following her line of logic, he'd not only removed his suit jacket, but he'd loosened his tie and rolled up the sleeves of his white shirt. His hair was just slightly disheveled. Though that should have given him a boyish look, his face was solemn, serious. His eyes were dark and smoky, almost as if they were absorbing the light being reflected from the fire in the fireplace.

Handing her a glass of brandy, he said, "That's very beautiful. You're very beautiful."

"Thank you," she said. Her gaze locked with his as she accepted the glass he gave her. Their hands met, fingers brushing for the few seconds it took to pass the brandy, and Julia got a quiver in the pit of her stomach that made her feel as if she'd made a big mistake.

Knowing she might be panicking prematurely, she sat on the white sofa. Brock sat beside her. "I was very proud of Zachary tonight. You should have been, too." He gave her a self-deprecating grin. "Actually, you should be much more proud of him than I am."

"I was...proud of him, I mean. And not more proud than you should be," she said, and truly meant it. "You deserve some credit with him, too, Brock. You've been so good to him. He looks up to you and respects you. He's tried to please you by behaving himself. You've gone a long way in motivating him."

Pleased, Brock chuckled, but as he did, Julia watched his arm stretch across the back of the sofa. Her tension climbed another notch. Anticipation quaked in her stomach. Not knowing what else to do, she brought her glass to her lips. As the warm brandy dripped to her tongue, she raised her gaze to meet Brock's, only to discover that once again they'd had the same idea. The smooth rim of his snifter lay pressed against his mouth. She could almost see the drop of brandy hit his tongue the same minute hers did. She felt the fire of the liquid and knew he felt it, too.

"This is ridiculous," she murmured, and set her glass on the coffee table.

Mimicking her movement, Brock also set his glass on the table. "I agree," he said, then gripped her upper arms and pulled her toward him. He gave her a second, only a second, to reconsider and change her mind, but locked in the prison of his smoky gaze, Julia couldn't look away or turn away. A thousand reasons pummeled her brain, reminding her that there was still a high possibility that this relationship had no future. But that niggling doubt, that one sacred possibility that he was growing comfortable here, that he was accepting his new position and a new life here, was much stronger than a million facts.

He kissed her.

Tremors exploded in her chest and radiated outward until she began to shiver. He released her upper arms in order to pull her more tightly against him, and she responded with the only sane thought in her head—to wrap her arms around him and hold on to him for dear life. No one had ever affected her as profoundly as he did. No one had ever made her quiver with need from a mere kiss, a light touch. She wasn't really sure what kind of hold he had over her, but one thing was certain, he had a hold.

It was more than attraction, though she found him attractive. More attractive than she'd ever found anyone. It was more than lust, though her insides had gone from warm to hot in a few seconds of kissing him. It was more than desire, though she certainly desired him. The thought of being intimate with this man, of sharing his secrets and his dreams, as well as sharing his bed, was like an unattainable dream. A grand dream. The ultimate dream. The kind of dream even a sane person would risk everything for.

Good God! She'd fallen in love with him.

The fact was enough to clear her emotion-filled thoughts and cause her to pull away from him because she knew if she didn't pull away now, she wouldn't be able to pull away at all. And she wasn't ready for the eventual outcome of the evening if she didn't go now.

"I really should go upstairs," she whispered, her voice shaky from the realization that she loved him, as much as from the fact that she'd risk almost anything for him. Except Zachary. His future. His dreams. His father's dreams for him. Those she wouldn't risk. But those weren't really in jeopardy right now. Her virtue was. Her emotions were. Even though she was ready to roll the dice with both, she wasn't quite ready to lose them yet. "I don't like to leave Zachary alone."

He released her, pulled back and stretched his arms comfortably across the back of the couch. "Okay, I understand."

"You do?" she said, breathless with relief. "Thank you."

"Don't mention it," he said as Julia quickly scrambled to make her getaway. But she got only as far as the doorway before he called to her again. "Julia."

She faced him. "Yes?"

"I'd like to take you to see the Connor place tomorrow. You know my father won't rest until you agree to take it. So at least come with me to take a look at it."

Losing herself in the dark pools of his brown eyes again, Julia realized both knew what he was really asking. He'd already admitted he wanted her in that house so they could have a chance to get to know each other. By asking him down here tonight, Julia as much as told him she also wanted a chance for them to get to know each other. She'd stopped their kiss because they were moving too fast. But without a place or a way to spend some private time together, they'd always be moving too fast, always be desperate.

She drew a long, quiet breath and expelled it slowly, soundlessly. "Okay."

Driving to the Connor house the next day, Julia felt her first stirrings of trepidation, but when she actually saw the house Brock and his father continually referred to as "old," she openly stared in awe. The two-story redbrick house was surrounded by bare brambles, the wiry branches of un-pruned rosebushes. The unkempt yard had a desolate look to it. But Julia didn't see that. She saw the house the way it would look in the summer, with the roses in full bloom, the yard neatly manicured, and the windows so clean they sparkled in the sun.

She never dreamed she'd live in a house this grand, let alone rent-free. A kind of guilt swept over her, but she remembered that she would be earning this as a salary of sorts. Though she'd never before been paid for being someone's friend, she understood Frank's motives very well. Putting her in this house kept her close. And that's what he wanted, someone to be close to, to be family with.

It seemed a pity he had to pay someone to be his family, but Julia was hoping that situation wouldn't last long. Because the biggest reason she was accepting this house wasn't to be Frank's family. She really would have done that without pay. The biggest reason she was accepting this house was to have that chance Brock kept talking about. Because if everything worked out the way she suspected, Frank wouldn't have to pay anyone to be his family anymore. Brock would come home.

Once in the house, Julia's vision of reality cleared. This close, it was hard not to see the two inches of dust, the cobwebs, the falling ceiling. Standing in the small foyer, she had a view of the empty dining room, living room and even the kitchen, which she could see through the open door at the end of the hall. She saw chipping paint and peeling wallpaper. She even saw a nasty water stain on the foyer wall, and she followed it the whole way into the dining room.

But potential was all around her, as well. The fireplace in the living room was crumbling, but Julia could see it crackling with a fire. She could see Zack's Christmas stocking hanging from the mantel. She saw heavy tapestry drapes, drawn back to reveal lightweight mauve sheers. She saw mauve carpeting, and comfortable, fat-cushioned furniture.

True, the thick white woodwork would have to be repainted, or scraped and then stained. The kitchen needed new cabinets. The dining room might have to be gutted. But there was potential, tons of potential, all around her.

Brock walked up behind her, slid his arms around her waist and rested his chin on the crown of her head. "I told you it needed work."

Far more concerned with the cost of renovating the house and the huge expense in terms of time than the repercussions of her actions, Julia turned in his arms. "Oh, Brock, are you sure you can afford it?"

He laughed merrily. "Julia, this is Roberts Run. I'll have contractors and subcontractors begging me to take their bids. We'll get good workmanship and we'll get it at a good price."

The fact that he spoke so highly of the town's craftspeople lifted her spirits so high, she lost herself to the moment. Springing to her tiptoes she kissed him lightly, then pulled away.

"I just hope your father thinks I'm worth all this."

Grabbing her wrist, Brock pulled her back into his arms again. "*I* think you're worth it. At the moment, that counts more than anything."

His declaration gave her a strange tingle of foreboding. He said it so lightly, so cavalierly, that she almost felt he was setting her up to be a mistress.

But she stopped those thoughts. Brock was happy, happier than she'd ever seen him, and she knew she was at least part of the reason. He wanted to get to know her. She wanted to get to know him. They'd set up the perfect way. If she panicked and said the wrong thing, she could insult him and ruin everything. Besides, she knew him well enough to know that he'd never do anything to compromise her reputation, let alone anything that would hurt her.

"Care to see the upstairs?" he asked quietly, but he was gazing into her eyes, communicating messages that were part devilish and part serious.

Knowing she was in over her head already, that they'd advanced too many levels too quickly, she stepped away from him. "Actually, we have enough to look at and think about down here," she said, pulling a small notebook from her jacket pocket. "Let's start in the dining room."

He caught her hand and pulled her against him again. "The dining room can wait."

He kissed her then. He didn't start slowly. He didn't lead her into the kiss with a few gentle nibbles. His mouth closed over hers, warm and hungry. And she met him. Because she loved him. Her doubts were quieted by pure, wanton need, but they were still there, and she knew she wouldn't be able to silence them forever.

Chapter Seventeen

"Come on, Julia," Frank sputtered. "I know this car goes a great deal faster than this. Otherwise, Brock wouldn't have spent almost a hundred grand for it."

"Frank," Julia said, gripping the steering wheel for dear life when she felt only two tires hug the road as she rounded one of the curves leading to Roberts Run. In the two weeks that had passed, she'd gone from riding in Brock's cars to driving them. But she wasn't an expert yet. "This car may be able to go much faster, but I don't drive well enough to let it. Relax. We'll be there in plenty of time."

Frank leaned against the door of the Mercedes with a grumble, and from the back seat Zack chanted, "Relax. Relax. Relax."

Julia knew he was only practicing a new vocabulary word, but she watched Frank's scowl deepen.

She laughed mercilessly. "Frank, we're going to be at least an hour early for the press conference. You'll have plenty of time to read over the speech Brock's written for you."

Frank sighed. "My company's expanding. We got a government contract four times the size of our normal workload. For the first time in thirty years, I'm taking on a huge block of new workers." He glanced at her. "For the first time *ever* I'm holding a press conference. And you want me to relax."

"Brock has everything under control," Julia reminded him, and couldn't help but smile. The whole world had never seemed brighter or better. While fixing up the Connor house, she and Brock had eased into a comfortable romantic relationship that wasn't going too fast or too slow. Moe had begun to drop by to visit Frank because he was tired of living his life for the diner. He and Frank were talking about fishing again. Frank was displaying life and enthusiasm the likes of which Julia had never seen. Then last night Brock came home with the news of the contract, the wonderful contract that wouldn't merely catapult Roberts Industries out of the red, it would bring work—and profits—for the next four years. And though Frank was complaining, Julia knew he was pleased. Very pleased. She settled back, slowing the Mercedes' speed so she could cruise into town.

Pulling into the parking lot, Julia saw evidence of construction crews everywhere. Sneaking a peek at Frank, she watched his expression change to one of complete awe as he took in the sight of his old brick factory being enlarged to accommodate the new work. She didn't say anything, simply let the reality soak in that his business had literally exploded.

As they walked into the reception area, the sound of the ringing phone competed with the sounds of the builders. Nadine held the phone receiver to one ear, while one finger in the other ear blocked out the noise of the construction crew. Frank only shook his head. Julia led him to the brand new elevator.

"I'm strong enough now that I could walk, you know."

"I know," Julia agreed, and guided him into the elevator, anyway. They rode up in silence, but Julia noticed his satisfied smirk as the shiny metal doors opened to allow their exit.

"Mr. Roberts!" Mary happily greeted as they stepped into her office.

"Mary," Frank said, then accepted her hug. "It's damned good to be back."

"It's damned good to have you back!" Mary said.

Frank scowled. "Brock been treating you poorly?"

"Oh, no!" Mary hastily assured him. "It's just that I like having you around, too."

Even as she said the last, Brock and Ian stepped out of Frank's office. Handing Ian a thick folder of papers, Brock said, "Give these figures one final run-through to be sure you haven't missed anything, then mail it off."

"You got it, Brock," Ian said happily, then turned and saw Julia and his father. "Hey, hi, Dad. Julia. Zack," he added, stooping to Zack's height to ruffle his hair. "Hey, nice suit."

"Thank you, Mr. Roberts," Zack said, then shyly ducked his head.

"So what's going on?" Frank asked as Ian left the room.

"Just exactly what I told you last night at dinner," Brock said, directing his dad into his office, at the same time catching Julia by the arm, kissing her hello and then lightly squeezing Zack's hand. "I bid on that contract because I knew no one else wanted it. It's small potatoes for most companies, but for Roberts Industries it's a godsend. That's why I had enough confidence to start renovations even before we got word of the award."

"All right," Frank agreed. "I'm with you so far. What I need to know is what you want me to say today."

"It's all here," Brock said, maneuvering Frank to take the chair behind the desk. Though Julia had never seen this office dirty or even slightly messy, today it virtually shined.

The tables had been dusted and were cleared of magazines. The bookcase had been reordered. The rug looked newly vacuumed. Obviously, this was where Frank would be meeting the press.

Guiding Zack to the sofa, she listened as Brock continued to explain the situation to his father.

"You give this short statement about winning the award and needing to hire new workers and looking forward to continued growth."

"Okay," Frank agreed, eyeing the statement as Brock looked on over his shoulder. "And how do I answer the questions about this future growth?"

"I want you to defer to Ian," Brock responded immediately. "I've given him a crash course in seeking out government requests for quotes and he knows our new capabilities. He's the best person to field questions on that one."

Frank relaxed in his chair. "What a relief."

Brock smiled. "I knew you'd be pleased."

As Brock stepped away from his father's chair, Frank caught his hand. "I am, Brock. I am pleased. What you've done here is remarkable."

"Dad, I didn't exactly get lucky, but I had knowledge from the work I do at Compu-Soft that put me in a position to do things here no one else could have done. I really don't think I deserve any praise. So, let's just continue on with your briefing."

"No. I'd like to take the conversation back a few paces," Arlen Johnson said from the office door. Wearing twill trousers and a white shirt, a slight departure from the typical navy blue uniform worn by the regular workers in the shop, Arlen stood in the doorway, holding a clipboard with some papers on it. He looked nervous, but determined, as if he had something on his mind and planned to say it.

Though Julia felt her heart freeze with anticipation, Brock merely nodded at Arlen and smiled. "I need to prepare my father for a press conference, Arlen," he politely said. "But I'll have plenty of time to discuss any problems you have this afternoon."

"I want to talk about them now, in front of your father."

"Arlen," Brock said, still the picture of patience. "I...*we* don't have time for this...."

"Yes, we do," Frank said, looking at Arlen with a speculative expression. "Come on in, Arlen. What's on your mind?"

Though he didn't argue or even look perturbed, Brock took a pace backward, as if deferring the conversation to his father. Whether he did that because he didn't want to deal with Arlen or out of respect for his father, Julia didn't know. She only knew she had an inescapable feeling that something bad was about to happen.

"Mr. Roberts, I'm sure I don't have to tell you that the rumors about the big contract are already out on the floor."

Frank chuckled. "My people are too smart not to realize something was in the air. I'm not surprised."

"Yeah, well," Arlen said, then he swallowed. Nervousness made his voice shake. "I...some of the guys and I...wanted a chance to tell Brock how much we appreciated that."

Julia felt a surge of relief, as well as a surge of empathy for Arlen because she knew how difficult that one brief statement had been for him to make, but Brock brushed it off casually. "As I just told my father, Arlen, I had some inside knowledge that gave me an edge. I didn't do anything special here."

"Yes, you did, Brock," Frank insisted, turning slightly in his thick leather chair to face his son. "This may not be a big deal to you, but to us it's the future." He turned his chair again. "Right, Arlen?"

"Yes, sir, it is."

"And we appreciate that," Frank added, then faced Arlen again. "Right, Arlen?"

"Yes, sir, we do."

Recognizing that Frank had said for Arlen what he'd come to say, Julia was slightly surprised when Arlen didn't leave. Frank gave him a few seconds to regroup, and when he didn't, Frank said, "Anything else on your mind, Arlen?"

Arlen cleared his throat. "I'd like to apologize to Brock."

"For what?" Frank asked glibly. "You two have a spat or something while I was gone?"

"We sort of had a disagreement a few years ago...."

"Water under the bridge," Brock interrupted, his expression softening. "It's forgotten."

Arlen visibly relaxed even as Julia felt herself visibly relax. He meant it. She knew Brock Roberts well enough to know that when he said something in that tone, with that look, he meant it. He really forgave Arlen Johnson. The past really was forgotten.

Suddenly, unexpectedly, Julia felt as if she were watching her whole life fall into place. Her heart felt buoyant, light. Now there was absolutely no reason for Brock to leave and every reason for him to stay. His company needed him, this town needed him. This town respected and admired him. Everything he wanted from this town was now his. Which meant every dream she ever had was about to come true.

Arlen turned to leave, but changed his mind and faced Frank and Brock again. When he spoke, he looked directly at Brock. "I also wanted to say that it's going to be a pleasure working for you."

Brock cleared his throat. "Well, Arlen, it has been a pleasure working with you, too, but I'm not staying on permanently at Roberts Industries. In fact, I'm going to be leaving very soon."

Arlen nodded and left the room, but Julia felt her stomach tighten. Her perfect life had lasted all of twenty seconds.

Frank spun his chair to face Brock. "You don't expect Ian and me to keep up with this brainstorm of yours, do you?"

"Dad, we all knew this wasn't permanent."

Brock spoke to his father, but Julia felt an odd sense that he was actually talking to her. Reminding her that if there was anything they'd continually discussed it was the fact that their relationship wasn't permanent.

"Surely you recognize Ian and I can't handle this by ourselves!" Frank barked, astonished. "My God, Brock, we're going to need an army to handle the paperwork alone."

"Precisely," Brock casually said. "You'll hire accountants, contact administrators, computer people. You don't need me."

"Really?" Frank all but bellowed. "Who the hell's going to organize all this?"

"I thought you were," Brock quietly told his father. "I thought you wanted to come back, that this company was like your baby. That's why I fixed it."

"Damn it, Brock! I was thinking about retiring. I wanted the company fixed so *you'd* stay home!"

Not even slightly repentant, Brock said, "I can't stay home. Compu-Soft was served with papers by a union yesterday. I can't let a union come in and organize while I'm nine hundred miles away. I don't care if the workers organize, but I want to be sure they don't get a bum deal if they do organize. I'm leaving for Boston tonight. You and Ian can handle what needs done here. My place is at Compu-Soft."

Chapter Eighteen

Shocked, Julia deflated on the sofa. Glancing at Brock, she saw him realize how his news had affected her. He turned to his father. "Watch Zack for a few minutes, would you?" he asked quietly.

"Sure, hell, why not? It might be the last time I get to see the little guy for the next year, since I'm going to be buried under paperwork."

"You're going to hire people to help you," Brock said simply while he helped Julia off the sofa. "And this time next year, you're going to be thrilled I gave you this opportunity."

"Don't count on it," Frank called as Brock pulled Julia through the office door and down the hall.

"Julia," Brock said, pressing the elevator button. The doors closed behind them, cocooning them in the small cubicle. "This is incredibly bad timing. I had hoped to break this news over dinner."

Numb, Julia only stared at him. "What? You think it's easier to get dumped over dinner than it is to get dumped in an office?" she asked. Saying nothing, Brock dragged her out of the elevator and then out of the building.

"You're not getting dumped," Brock said, laughing as he led her out into the parking lot. "We have exactly ten minutes to have this discussion, so I don't want your answer or anything like that. I just want you to objectively listen to my plan. Okay?"

He sounded so positive, Julia nodded optimistically. They found a secluded corner that wasn't being bulldozed, hammered or added to, and Brock leaned against the wall, pulling Julia to him.

He kissed her once, long and lingeringly, before he said, "I have to go back to Compu-Soft. I want to be certain my workers get a good union. I'm the one who has to look out for my people. I can't desert them now."

"All right," Julia agreed, understanding that logic. "I see what you're saying. You feel as strongly about the Compu-Soft employees as your father feels about the Roberts Industries people. I can deal with your wanting to protect them. Just tell me when you'll be back, and I'll adjust."

He took a long breath. "I'm not coming back. Not permanently. Not to run Roberts Industries. And not even for a visit until about Thanksgiving."

Her heart stopped. "Thanksgiving?"

"Julia, I've already been away for two months. Compu-Soft needs me. It'll take me two months to wade through the union proceedings and then four months to get my regular work caught up...if I ever get caught up."

She stepped away from him. "I see."

He grabbed her hand and pulled her back again. "That's why I want you to come with me."

"Come with you?"

"To Boston."

She gaped at him. "Boston?"

"Now, before you get all hyper on me, hear me out. My life is not as bright and brilliant as everybody thinks it is.

Except for a few outdoor sports, I'm a homebody. If and when I entertain, it's only friends—friends who will adore you. You will fit into my life perfectly, beautifully."

Giving him a few seconds to elaborate, Julia stayed quiet. When he didn't add anything to that, she said, "I'll fit in beautifully, as what?"

"As my companion," Brock said. "You know we belong together," he said, and from the tone of his voice, Julia knew he meant it. But sincere or not, those words were a far cry from the words she'd been wanting to hear for the last two weeks. "I think you also know I'll make a good father for Zack."

Confused, she licked her dry lips, then said, "That might be true, Brock, but it almost seems as if you haven't heard a word I've said to you over the past six weeks."

Puzzled, he looked at her. "What's that supposed to mean?"

"It means, I really do believe I should raise Zack in Roberts Run. It means, I genuinely believe that would be David's wish. It means, I don't *want* to go to Boston."

"So David's wishes are more important than mine?"

"At this point, Brock, that's really not even an issue. The real issue," she said, looking into his eyes and wondering how he could be so dense, "is that I cannot live with you and expect to keep the Whittakers from zooming into court to take Zachary away from me...away from us."

His expression turned incredulous. "Are you telling me that after six weeks of knowing each other, you think I should *marry* you?"

A slap in the face would have hurt less than the tone of his voice. She lifted her chin. "I'm telling you that after four weeks we made a commitment to get to know each other and you're breaking it after only two."

"I think we know each other well enough."

She tilted her head. "To live together, but not to be married."

"I haven't actually asked you to live with me in the sense that you mean," he pointed out cautiously. "After all, you've kept us at more than an arm's distance. And," he added a little more aggressively, "as far as I'm concerned, your virtue is still intact."

"And that bothers you."

He drew a long breath. "In a way, yes."

"Brock, surely you see that I have to be on good behavior or Zack's grandparents will have the grounds they need to take Zack away from me."

"I think you're wrong," Brock said emphatically. "This is the nineties, Julia, not the fifties. Not only is living together a perfectly acceptable way to test a relationship before committing to marriage, but if you and Zack were living with me no court could possibly find that he wasn't being well cared for. He'd have good schools, a comfortable life and a wonderful home."

Again, she waited for Brock to add more. One simple phrase, or maybe one little word. Anything, as long as it related to love. At this point, if he even said he loved Zack, Julia would take it as a good sign. But if he couldn't admit to loving a child as irresistible as Zack, and he couldn't admit to loving her, then the conversation was becoming moot. Not because she wouldn't move to Boston with him—couldn't, it was too much of a risk—but because his not having any plans for even *visiting* until November almost proved he didn't have any deep and lasting feelings for her.

While she, on the other hand, had fallen in love.

When a full thirty seconds ticked off without another word from Brock, Julia said, "Do you realize, Brock, that those are all the things the Whittakers are already offering us, and they're things I've already decided to turn down?"

"This is different."

Hoping, pushing the envelope because she was desperate, Julia asked, "How is your offer different from what the Whittakers are offering? They put good schools and a good home on the table six weeks ago. How is living with you so different?''

She felt him tense. "Julia, I'm not going to marry you after knowing you only six weeks.''

"I'm not really sure I want to marry you after six weeks, either, Brock,'' Julia said, then she swallowed hard. She had to draw the line somewhere and this was it. If he hadn't gotten the hint of what she wanted to hear by now, then he didn't love her. Empty, she brought the conversation back to its logical conclusion. "But I do know I won't risk Zachary's future by living with you."

"Then, we're through," he said, sounding incredulous. He combed his fingers through his hair. "I can't believe this.''

"I can't, either," Julia said, looking up at him. Shoving her pride to the farthest corner of her brain, she said, "Particularly since all you have to do is come home every once in a while to visit."

That seemed to affect him as profoundly as a punch in the stomach. For several seconds he only stared at her, then he said, "Don't you dare blame this on me. I gave you everything you wanted for the past six weeks. Treated you like a princess. And the first time I really ask for anything from you, you refused. You, Julia, not me."

"What you're asking isn't exactly simple, Brock."

"Yes, it is," he said, still looking at her as if she were crazy. "We belong together. We're good together. We even need each other in a sort of odd way. But you're so damn stubborn, you refuse to see that. Not because you can't understand that what I'm asking *is* possible, but because you don't want to leave Roberts Run."

Julia's tongue began to form the words to argue, but she realized she couldn't. He was right. She didn't want to leave. Everything she'd ever had was here. Everything she wanted to give her son was here.

In the end, she said nothing, and Brock again combed his fingers through his hair. "Great. Fine," he said. "I've got the whole picture now. But let me tell you something, Julia. You might be well advised to take the Whittakers up on their offer of living with them, because the way I see it, you don't have any idea of what you're throwing away because you've never tried any other way to live except living here. And for all you know, you might have just made the biggest mistake of your life."

This time, *he* stepped away from *her*. Julia felt the loss as a physical pain because he really didn't understand. He didn't see that not one word of love had passed between them.

Confused, she stood by the quiet wall. By the time she realized Brock was walking away from her, he was almost inside the building.

He didn't wait for her to catch up to him, merely walked into his father's office, assembled his belongings and headed for the door again. Julia passed him as she entered, but he didn't say a word, only walked right by her.

Even as her heart splintered with pain, her pride forced it back together again. She wouldn't risk Zack for anybody. Particularly not for a man who couldn't promise her anything more than a wonderful house, good schools and a comfortable life.

Not a happy life. Not a life full of love and laughter. Just a comfortable life.

Chapter Nineteen

Brock entered the Compu-Soft offices and was immediately greeted by Norm, the security guard. "Mr. Roberts," he said joyfully, rising from his seat behind the half-moon desk. Norm's voice echoed hollowly in the huge glass foyer because there was nothing in the foyer save for Norm's desk. A bank of elevators lined the back wall, but a set of three steps off to the right went to the corridor that led to the first floor offices. Brock had designed the building this way to preclude visitors—potential competitors—from even inadvertently catching a glimpse of the inner workings of Compu-Soft. The only offices on this floor were a mail room and a supply room, both of which were behind closed doors.

Funny, but until today, that had seemed like such a good idea. Brock had no clue why it didn't seem like a good idea to him today. He only knew that it didn't.

"It's sure as hell good to have you back," Norm said, breaking Brock from his reverie.

"It's sure as hell good to be back," Brock said, and took the hand Norm extended for shaking. "I feel like I'm coming home."

"You are home, sir," Norm said, scrambling to get the elevator button for Brock, though Brock had nothing more than a briefcase in his hand and could have easily managed the button himself. With a nod, he thanked Norm for the kindness, and entered the elevator. "See you at lunch," he called.

"Yes, sir, Mr. Roberts," Norm shouted back. "You just buzz down here ten minutes before you want to leave for lunch and I'll make sure Jimmy gets your car."

The elevator doors closed and Brock inhaled the scent of his own building, his own company, his domain. In spite of the union problems awaiting his return, the most wonderful sense of peace and security settled over him. He luxuriated in that feeling until the elevator slowed to a stop, the bell sounded and the doors silently slid open.

He entered a corridor of oak wainscoting and hardwood floors, the look and feel of wood interrupted only by the three Oriental rugs that led to the oak double doors at the end of the hall.

His office.

Confused, he glanced around. He remembered once telling Julia his life was much simpler in Boston; that he hadn't inherited his mother's ornate taste. And though it was true, his building wasn't ornate, it was obviously expensive. Tasteful, but expensive. Ornate in a sophisticated, almost pretentious kind of way.

He shook his head as if to clear a haze. He knew what was wrong. Like a fool, he was seeing this building, his life, through Julia's eyes, and it was crazy. She was wrong. He didn't want to go back. And she was the fool for not seeing that she'd fit in here every bit as well as he did. She was also a fool for not giving Zachary the chance to live this kind of life with him.

The second he opened the door to his office, the sound of party horns erupted. His core staff, the men and women who'd been with him since he took over the company, stood gathered around the desk of his administrative assistant, Gloria. Each and every one of them wore a silly party hat. Harvy, the comptroller, held a huge cake. The only thing missing was confetti, and Brock got the strangest, most uncomfortable feeling that if they weren't so worried about neatness and order, they'd have had confetti, too.

Deliberately unwrinkling his brow, Brock set his briefcase on the floor and opened his arms. "Thank you," he said happily. "Thank you very much. This is wonderful."

"It's great to have you back," Harvy said. "And don't worry, we're taking this cake down to the cafeteria with the other cakes we bought for the entire crew. We'll actually be eating down there."

"No, sit down," Brock said, motioning for them to stop, since they'd already begun to disperse. "We'll call the cafeteria for a pot of coffee and you guys can help me catch up while we have some cake."

For a full thirty seconds, everyone looked too stunned to respond, then Gloria cleared her throat. "Well, that would be fine, but I have an itinerary made, Brock. Everybody got their usual fifteen-minute slot for a meeting with you in your private conference room." She grimaced. "Besides, I don't think we really want to risk getting chocolate cake crumbs on that gray carpet."

"I have been living with more than crumbs over the past few weeks," Brock said with a chuckle. "My father hired a practical nurse... well, she wasn't really a practical nurse. She was the town's waitress, but she needed to spend some time in our house because her son was about to meet his paternal grandparents. Zachary was always just slightly dirty and running...."

Seeing how oddly everyone was staring at him, Brock stopped short. It wasn't that they were disinterested in what he had to say, it was more that they seemed astounded that he was talking to them about something personal.

And they were right.

Good Lord, he'd never babbled to these people before, and, if he didn't stop, they were going to think he was crazy. "Anyway, it was a long, grueling trip...." Actually, it hadn't been. It had been a ray of sunshine. True, it was rough going in the beginning, but in the end, he'd felt very good about going home. He'd mended fences, made his peace with the past, even grown to love Roberts Run for what it was. And he'd done most of that because Julia had forced him to face his demons, to talk about his life even though he hadn't wanted to.

He shook his head as if to clear a haze. It didn't matter. He was here now. And this was his home. This was where he belonged.

"Let me see that itinerary, Gloria, and let's get this boat out on the ocean again."

His entire staff seemed to breathe a sigh of relief, which came out as something like a halfhearted chuckle, then they dispersed like children at the sound of a school bell. The morning was quickly eaten up by meetings, and at twelve o'clock Gloria came into the conference room and announced that Jimmy, the parking lot attendant, had brought Brock's Jaguar around to the front of the building. She also told him she'd made arrangements for him to have lunch at a small exclusive restaurant with two of his golfing buddies—since the season was already upon them—and she wanted to know if Brock wanted a racket ball court for that evening.

"I think I'll be unpacking tonight," Brock said as he slid into his top coat.

"But you always play racket ball on Thursdays," Gloria said, confused. "Besides, I made arrangements for Martha to be at your house tomorrow to restock your refrigerator and do your laundry. She'll unpack for you."

"Oh, okay," Brock said. "Book the racket ball court."

Pleased, Gloria smiled. "See you at two."

He turned. "Two?"

"Well, when you have lunch with Sam and Alan you always come back at two."

"And, tell me, Gloria, what do I order?"

That stung. Visibly hurt, she stepped back a pace.

"I'm sorry," Brock apologized immediately. "I'd plead jet lag, but I drove. I guess I'm just tired."

"And you should be," Gloria said, placating him. "You left one company full of problems and returned to another. You've got your work cut out for you. That's why you should have your two-hour lunch and take advantage of your exercise tonight. You'll feel better tomorrow."

"Probably," Brock agreed, then left for lunch. But he didn't feel any better the next day. Or even the rest of the week. Twice in those long, lonely seven days, he picked up the phone to call Julia, if only to tell her about his life, about the problems he was facing. Both times he replaced the receiver without dialing her number. He knew what calling her meant—a commitment—and he couldn't do it. He didn't want to give up what he had. His friends, his life, the company that made his name and reputation.

With every day that passed, though, he missed her a little more. He couldn't sleep, he didn't want to eat, and the problems of Compu-Soft seemed smaller and increasingly irrelevant, until one day he simply walked out of a staff meeting.

At seven o'clock that night, he was sitting in his office, staring out the huge wall of windows at the lights of Boston. Like it or not, he'd figured out what was wrong. Life here wasn't fun. It wasn't even slightly interesting. There were no surprises. Not one person ever argued with him. Hell, no one even questioned anything he said. And not one of them ever entered his conference room without a jacket. The men all wore ties. The women buttoned their blouses to mid-throat. He couldn't picture any one of them in torn jeans and a rumpled sweatshirt—without shoes, without combing their hair—daring him to comment on their attire. Shaking his head in wonder, Brock squeezed his eyes shut. God, he missed her.

"If you don't mind, Mr. Roberts," Gloria said, poking her head through the open doorway. "I'm going home."

"Oh, God, Gloria, I'm sorry," Brock apologized, glancing at his watch. "I had no idea you were still here."

"I know. You were pretty deep in thought."

Brock nodded. "Yeah."

"Well, good night."

"Good night," Brock said. He turned to stare out the window, but changed his mind and faced Gloria again. Two seconds before she would have pulled the door closed, he said, "Gloria, has my life always been this crazy?"

She stared at him. "I think your life is very organized."

"I'm not talking about organization, I'm talking about the way everything happens around here."

She straightened to her full five-feet-two-inch height. Obviously still defensive about Brock walking out of the staff meeting without explanation. "We're all very organized around here."

"Has anyone ever told you you're too organized?" he asked seriously.

She burst out laughing. "Certainly not you," she said, then timidly made her way into his office. Slowly edging onto one of the chairs in front of his desk, she said, "Anything you want to talk about? I know your father almost died. I know that sometimes changes people." She shrugged. "If there's anything on your mind, I wouldn't mind listening."

Confused, Brock threw his pencil to his desk. "Gloria, I used to love it here. I made this company exactly the way I thought a company should be made."

"And you were right. We're very successful. And very happy. Most of us are more secure than we ever were in any other job. I, personally," she said, pointing at her chest, "believe this is the best-run company in the world. I wouldn't want to work anywhere else. I'm very content. Beyond content. This is where I'm supposed to be."

"Then why am I so unhappy?"

She smiled sheepishly. "Jet lag?"

Brock ruefully returned her smile. "I drove, remember?"

"I'm not a psychologist, Brock," Gloria said, then rose from her chair. "But my guess is you liked running the family business better than you like running this one. Or maybe you enjoyed the challenge of revamping that company, making it as good as you've made this one."

"Maybe."

"Or maybe you just miss the practical nurse-waitress with the little boy...Zachary."

He smiled. "Maybe."

"So go home," Gloria said, and turned toward the door. "To your real home. You've sold off all that stock, and there's a new board of directors coming in, anyway. You'll still be chairman, but there's no better time than right now to pick a new president."

Brock glanced up from his desk. "Harvy?" he asked quietly.

Gloria turned, smiled. "Harvy's a good choice. A great choice. I think I'd enjoy working for Harvy."

"I'm going to see to it you get a raise before I go."

"You can count on that one," she said, then closed the door.

Brock leaned back in his chair. He might be able to go home to Roberts Run. He'd probably get control of the company away from his father with nothing more than a good riddance. But he wasn't really sure he'd get Julia back again. There had been one too many cross words, one too many insults. And the funny part of it was, he wasn't even sure what they were. Which meant he couldn't really be sure he could fix whatever was wrong.

Chapter Twenty

Brock arrived at his father's house a little after ten the next morning. Everything was so quiet, he got an eerie feeling, but he squelched it. He laid his garment bag across the banister of the spiral staircase and then walked upstairs. Pausing outside of Julia's room, he drew a long breath for courage then knocked twice.

"She's not here," Brock's father said from behind him.

Brock spun around. "Dad! What are you doing here? Why aren't you at work?"

"I'm on half days, remember?" he said. "Oh, that's right, you wouldn't remember. You're the guy who made eight times the workload for me instead of helping me cut my workload in half like the doctor said. Poor Ian's about nuts. We're hiring a personnel director this week so he can hire enough staff to at least stay even. He has no illusions about getting ahead of things."

"Yeah, well," Brock said. "I'm home. And for good. So, I'll help Ian hire the personnel manager. Right now, I just need to know where Julia is."

Frank caught Brock's arm. "You're home? For good?"

"For good," Brock said, then patted his father's shoulder. "It seems I missed this place, after all."

"Are you sure it wasn't that you missed Julia?" Frank asked.

"*That*, I'm not ready to talk about just yet."

"Well, you might as well talk about it with me. You're not going to get to talk about it with Julia. She left. She's gone to Connecticut."

"But she wasn't supposed to go for another three weeks!"

"She told me she was feeling strong," Frank said, then turned away. "That she'd made some really big decisions and she was ready to go. She said there was no point in putting off the inevitable."

"What kind of decisions and what kind of inevitable are we talking about here, Dad?"

"Well, Brock, something you said about raising Zack the right way must have hit home. She told me she's going to give living with Zack's grandparents a fair shake."

Brock's heart stopped. "Oh, no," he said, squeezing the bridge of his nose with his thumb and index finger. "Get me the address for the Whittakers, I'm going up there."

"Don't have it," Frank said, then walked away with a satisfied smile. "Think your way out of this one, Princeton graduate."

When Zachary awoke, Julia already had them halfway across the Pennsylvania Turnpike. "Well, hello there, sleepyhead," Julia said, looking at her son through the rearview mirror. "We have about six miles to the next rest stop," she told him. "Do you think you can wait another ten minutes before you go to the bathroom?"

Zachary looked at her through sleep-heavy eyes. "Uh-huh."

"Okay, but if you really need to go, you tell Mommy, because we can always stop alongside the road."

"Okay."

She continued to watch Zack in her rearview mirror, waited for him to say something else, but he didn't. Returning her gaze to the road, Julia sighed. Never in his entire life had Zachary been a quiet child, but since Brock had left the Roberts home, Zack had hardly made more than a two-word sentence. She knew exactly how he felt. She missed Brock, too. She missed the way he argued with her without putting her down. She missed the way he looked at her. She missed the way her heart skipped a beat whenever he was around. She missed the way it felt to be held in his arms....

But she was sticking by her guns. A man who couldn't say he loved her, didn't love her. Period.

Even as she thought the last, Julia knew it wasn't true. He did love her. She knew it. The real problem was, he couldn't admit it. And that was a worse problem than not being able to love. Because he could fool himself, protect himself for the rest of his life if he wanted. He was strong enough, smart enough, to do that. If a crisis the size of his moving nine hundred miles away hadn't gotten him to break the barriers, they weren't going to be broken. Julia had to deal with that. No matter how much it hurt. And it did hurt. There were times it hurt so much all she wanted to do was roll in a ball and cry. But she couldn't. She had a son to raise and grandparents to integrate into Zack's life with as much ease as possible. She didn't have the time or the luxury to give in to her misery. Difficult though it was to fight it, she fought it.

They reached the rest stop more quickly than Julia had anticipated and she breathed a sigh of relief. "Here we are, Zack. Just hold on for a couple more minutes."

He didn't answer, but then again she really didn't expect him to. Though he was groggy from his nap, he was still in a mourning of sorts and Julia didn't push him. She knew exactly how he felt. She parked her car, pulled Zack out of his car seat and began walking toward the busy rest stop building. Because it was a warm day, travelers were clustered outside. Some ate ice cream or sipped soft drinks, while others simply soaked up the sun and enjoyed the opportunity to be out of their cars.

Straightening her comfortable white T-shirt and fluffing out her travel-worn hair, Julia led Zack to the main building. She'd chosen to make this trip in loose-fitting jeans and a T-shirt and had dressed Zack the same way. Now that she'd grown accustomed to dressing up a level, she almost felt out of place in such casual clothes. But she and Zack would be driving all day and had another day of driving ahead of them. Making the trip in uncomfortable clothes would be foolish, and Julia had decided she was done being foolish. She was who she was—perhaps a little more polished and poised now—but she was still herself. She was raising Zack to the best of her ability. The Whittakers would just have to accept that.

Ironically, now that she was strong enough to beat them, Julia had the uncanny feeling she wasn't going to have to fight them. There was safety in confidence, something dealing with Brock had taught her.

Her heart tightened. She really had to stop thinking about him. After all, she'd never see him again. He was strong enough that he could stay away forever if he wanted to. Forgetting about him should be downright easy.

Too bad it wasn't.

"Okay, Zack," she said, hoisting him into her arms to avoid the confusion of the bustling lobby. "Let's go to the bathroom." She pushed her way through the noisy crowd and was almost at the bathroom door when someone grabbed her upper arm. She got the oddest tingle, part fear and part something she couldn't define or describe, and she gripped Zack as tightly as she could.

"Excuse me, ma'am, but you're not taking that little boy into a ladies' room, are you?"

The achingly familiar voice stopped her heart.

"Here," Brock said, turning Julia to face him as he pulled Zack from Julia's arms. "I'm not having him grow up mentally distorted from too many trips into the women's bathroom. I'll take him into the men's room where he belongs."

With that Brock disappeared with her child and Julia found herself standing alone and disoriented, being pushed and bumped and jostled by the crowd in the huge room. It seemed like only seconds before Brock and Zack returned, and when they did Zack was holding an ice cream cone. Still perched on Brock's arm, Zack held his frozen treat precariously close to Brock's hair, though Brock seemed to neither notice nor care.

The second they were near enough, Julia grabbed Zack. "I'll take him now and we'll be on our way."

Brock caught her arm again. "Give me five minutes."

She pulled free. "You've already had almost two months."

She turned and began walking out of the building, but Brock was right beside her. When they reached the glass-door entrance, he pushed it open for her.

"Two months is hardly long enough to get used to a lifestyle change, let alone admit it's time to come home."

"Don't congratulate yourself on finally realizing your father needs you," Julia said, bustling to her car. "You should have figured that out long ago."

"Well, I didn't," Brock said, opening the door so that Julia could slip Zack into his car seat. "I'm not slow and I'm not stupid, Julia. I simply had to find my own way...or maybe my own place in life. I'm not going to apologize for that."

"Peachy. Now, excuse me," she said, and reached for her car door.

Brock covered it with his hand, preventing her from opening it. "I'm not taking over Roberts Industries. But I am going to act as an administrative vice president and serve on the board. I'm going to do the same thing at Compu-Soft.''

"And I should care because…?'' Julia sarcastically said as she shielded her eyes from the sun with her hand. Her recently grown nails had been painted pink. Her hands— which hadn't been soaked in dishwater every day for the past two months—had returned to their natural smoothness. Even though she had Brock and Frank to thank for that, Julia still wasn't giving an inch. He wasn't going to hurt her again. She wasn't going to let him.

"You just can't let this be easy, can you.''

"No, I can't, Brock. I'm a very simple woman with very simple needs. I don't run a twenty million dollar company. I don't go to the symphony. I wouldn't know a four-star restaurant if it bit me in the ankle. We don't speak the same language. I'm not taking any chances on not understanding you again.''

He sighed, glanced at the sky, then looked down at her again. "Then I'll spell it out for you. I'm not making my permanent home in Boston. I'm going to live in Roberts Run. In fact, I'd like to live in the old Connor place.''

Julia turned away from him. "Fine. Consider it yours.'' Caught off guard, Brock couldn't stop her when she reached for the car door again. She managed to pull it open, but he slammed it closed.

"I want to live there with you.''

That stopped her heart, but she didn't turn around. She straightened her spine and lifted her chin. "I learned my lesson on that one,'' she said quietly, glancing at Zack, who was in the back seat of Moe's car, sitting in the car seat, dripping ice cream everywhere. "I told you I'm not *living with* anybody.''

"It's going to look really foolish to the people in town for us to get married and not live together.''

She didn't say anything. Wouldn't turn around. Wouldn't look at him.

"Julia," Brock said quietly, soothingly, "the time I spent in Boston was hell."

Voice quivering, Julia said, "You shouldn't have left your father alone. He missed you. That's what makes him ineffective and overgenerous. He just wants people to like him."

"I know that now. And even though I missed my father probably as much as he missed me, I didn't miss him half as much as I missed you . . . and Zack," he added.

When she didn't say anything, Brock took her upper arms and turned her to face him. "Say anything," he commanded softly. "Yell at me, scream at me, tell me I told you so. Just say something."

"I can't," Julia said, not looking at him. "I think I'm in shock."

"Does this mean you agree?" Brock asked hopefully. Putting one finger beneath her chin, he lifted her face. He kissed her once, softly, and Julia felt all her bones begin to melt. After so many years of being alone, with only one sweet taste of what it had been like to have someone who loved her, she finally had a second chance to be loved.

Or so she thought . . .

"Actually, no," she said, and pulled away from him. "At least not yet."

He swallowed. This was it, the impasse. The thing he hadn't figured out yet. With a heavy sigh, he decided to admit it. "Julia, just like you told me, we have a communication block and you aren't taking anything for granted. Well, I'm going to admit that our communication block has me stymied right now because I haven't the slightest idea what you want from me. I only know I love you and I want to marry you. Whatever else you want, you're going to have to tell me."

Though tears gathered in the corners of Julia's eyes, she smiled. "That was it. I wanted you to tell me you loved me."

He stared at her. "That was it?"

She nodded.

"You didn't already know?" he asked incredulously.

She shook her head. "No, you have to say it."

"I'm saying it," he said, and bent his head and kissed her. "I love. I love you. I love you."

She smiled at him. "I love you, too, but are you really sure you want to do this?"

He kissed her. "Positive."

She pulled away again. "You're not going to grow bored in Roberts Run?"

"No, I'm not. Because we're going to be taking Zack to visit his grandparents frequently enough to appease them ... because I personally feel they'd miss a really good deal if they didn't get to know this child." He looked in at Zack, and Julia watched ice-cream-faced Zack grin back at him.

"Yes, they would," Julia agreed.

"And when I go to Boston to handle things for Compu-Soft, I'm going to expect you to come with me."

Julia only stared at him. "To do what?"

"To shop for clothes for our kids while I'm working, and to attend the symphony or ballet with me when I'm not."

"I suppose I could learn to do that."

"You are a quick study," Brock agreed, then brushed his lips across hers lightly. "And to make love three or four times a day in our apartment in Boston, because Mrs. Thomas has agreed to become our children's nanny, and she and my dad will be keeping the kids when we go away."

"What's your dad going to do for a cook?"

Brock laughed. "Moe's giving up the diner. He's going to cook for my father and the two of them are going to start fishing again."

"But who's going to run the diner?"

"I heard Arlen Johnson's buying it."

At that Julia laughed lightly.

"You could put your arms around me and give me a real hug," Brock said. "I've never felt as deserted and alone as I have in the past week, and a little human comfort would go a long way."

Slipping her arms along his neck, Julia sighed with contentment. "You'll be getting all the human comfort you can handle in the next fifty years."

"Yeah, but I could use a little human comfort *now,* and I don't mean two weeks from now when you get home from the Whittakers'."

"Well, we do have a one-night hotel stay on the way to Connecticut. If you wanted to drive up with us, we could make good use of that time. I'm sure the Whittakers would be glad to meet my future husband...."

"What about Zack?"

Julia smiled. "If you keep him amused and don't let him nap the afternoon away in his car seat, he'll fall into a dead sleep tonight and won't even know we're in the room."

Without a word, Brock opened the door of the back seat. "Okay, Zack, we're going to play a little game my father taught me when we were traveling."

Zack patted Brock's cheek with an ice-cream-covered hand. Brock promptly removed the soggy cone from him and passed it out the window to Julia. "Take this to a trash can and find me a baby wipe."

"Baby wipes are in the glove compartment," Julia said, then walked the wet cone to a trash receptacle. The sun still beat down on the exposed skin of her arms, but now it felt warmer somehow, more comfortable.

For the first time in her life she was about to make a home, a real home, because she had a family.

And so did Zachary.

* * * * *

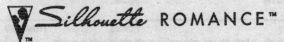

Take 4 bestselling love stories FREE

Plus get a FREE surprise gift!

Special Limited-time Offer

Mail to Silhouette Reader Service®

> P.O. Box 609
> Fort Erie, Ontario
> L2A 5X3

YES! Please send me 4 free Silhouette Romance™ novels and my free surprise gift. Then send me 6 brand-new novels every month, which I will receive months before they appear in bookstores. Bill me at the low price of $3.00 each plus 25¢ delivery and GST*. That's the complete price and a savings of over 10% off the cover prices—quite a bargain! I understand that accepting the books and gift places me under no obligation ever to buy any books. I can always return a shipment and cancel at any time. Even if I never buy another book from Silhouette, the 4 free books and the surprise gift are mine to keep forever.

315 BPA A3UX

Name	(PLEASE PRINT)	
Address	Apt. No.	
City	Province	Postal Code

This offer is limited to one order per household and not valid to present Silhouette Romance™ subscribers. *Terms and prices are subject to change without notice. Canadian residents will be charged applicable provincial taxes and GST.

CSROM-696   ©1990 Harlequin Enterprises Limited

This October, be the first to read these wonderful
authors as they make their dazzling debuts!

THE WEDDING KISS by Robin Wells
(Silhouette Romance #1185)
A reluctant bachelor rescues the woman he loves
from the man she's about to marry—and turns into
a willing groom himself!

THE SEX TEST by Patty Salier
(Silhouette Desire #1032)
A pretty professor learns there's more to making love
than meets the eye when she takes lessons from
a sexy stranger.

IN A FAMILY WAY by Julia Mozingo
(Special Edition #1062)
A woman without a past finds shelter in the arms of
a handsome rancher. Can she trust him to protect
her unborn child?

UNDER COVER OF THE NIGHT by Roberta Tobeck
(Intimate Moments #744)
A rugged government agent encounters the woman he has
always loved. But past secrets could threaten their future.

DATELESS IN DALLAS by Samantha Carter
(Yours Truly)
A hapless reporter investigates how to find the perfect
mate—and winds up falling for her handsome rival!

Don't miss the brightest stars of tomorrow!

Only from **Silhouette®**

The Calhoun Saga continues...

in November
New York Times bestselling author

NORA ROBERTS

takes us back to the Towers and introduces us to
the newest addition to the Calhoun household,
sister-in-law Megan O'Riley in

MEGAN'S MATE
(Intimate Moments #745)

And in December
look in retail stores for the special collectors'
trade-size edition of

THE
Calhoun
Women

containing all four fabulous Calhoun series books:
COURTING CATHERINE,
A MAN FOR AMANDA, FOR THE LOVE OF LILAH
and *SUZANNA'S SURRENDER.*
Available wherever books are sold.

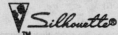

As seen on TV!
Free Gift Offer

With a Free Gift proof-of-purchase from any Silhouette® book,
you can receive a beautiful cubic zirconia pendant.

This gorgeous marquise-shaped stone is a genuine cubic
zirconia—accented by an 18" gold tone necklace.

(Approximate retail value $19.95)

Send for yours today...
compliments of ▼ *Silhouette*®

To receive your free gift, a cubic zirconia pendant, send us one original proof-of-purchase, photocopies not accepted, from the back of any Silhouette Romance™, Silhouette Desire®, Silhouette Special Edition®, Silhouette Intimate Moments® or Silhouette Yours Truly™ title available in August, September or October at your favorite retail outlet, together with the Free Gift Certificate, plus a check or money order for $1.65 U.S./$2.15 CAN. (do not send cash) to cover postage and handling, payable to Silhouette Free Gift Offer. We will send you the specified gift. Allow 6 to 8 weeks for delivery. Offer good until October 31, 1996 or while quantities last. Offer valid in the U.S. and Canada only.

Free Gift Certificate

Name: _____

Address: _____

City: _____ State/Province: _____ Zip/Postal Code: _____

Mail this certificate, one proof-of-purchase and a check or money order for postage and handling to: SILHOUETTE FREE GIFT OFFER 1996. In the U.S.: 3010 Walden Avenue, P.O. Box 9077, Buffalo NY 14269-9077. In Canada: P.O. Box 613, Fort Erie, Ontario L2Z 5X3.

FREE GIFT OFFER   084-KMD
ONE PROOF-OF-PURCHASE
To collect your fabulous FREE GIFT, a cubic zirconia pendant, you must include this
original proof-of-purchase for each gift with the properly completed Free Gift Certificate.

084-KMD

The collection of the year!
NEW YORK TIMES BESTSELLING AUTHORS

Linda Lael Miller
Wild About Harry

Janet Dailey
Sweet Promise

Elizabeth Lowell
Reckless Love

Penny Jordan
Love's Choices

and featuring
Nora Roberts
The Calhoun Women

This special trade-size edition features four of the wildly
popular titles in the Calhoun miniseries together in
one volume—a true collector's item!

Pick up these great authors and a chance to win
a weekend for two in New York City at the
Marriott Marquis Hotel on Broadway! We'll pay
for your flight, your hotel—even a Broadway show!

Available in December at your favorite retail outlet.

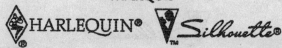

You're About to Become a *Privileged Woman*

Reap the rewards of fabulous free gifts and benefits with proofs-of-purchase from Silhouette and Harlequin books

Pages & Privileges™

It's our way of thanking you for buying our books at your favorite retail stores.

PROOF OF PURCHASE
Offer expires October 31, 1996
SR-PP189

Harlequin and Silhouette— the most privileged readers in the world!

For more information about Harlequin and Silhouette's PAGES & PRIVILEGES program call the Pages & Privileges Benefits Desk: 1-503-794-2499

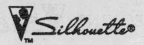

Silhouette®

SR-PP189